The Banner Boy
SCOUTS AFLOAT

The Secret of Cedar Island

GEORGE A. WARREN

1st WORLD
LIBRARY
Literary Society

The Banner Boy Scouts Afloat

George A. Warren

© 1st World Library – Literary Society, 2006
PO Box 2211
Fairfield, IA 52556
www.1stworldlibrary.org
First Edition

LCCN: 2006905699

Softcover ISBN: 1-4218-2128-1
Hardcover ISBN: 1-4218-2028-5
eBook ISBN: 1-4218-2228-8

Purchase *"The Banner Boy Scouts Afloat"*
as a traditional bound book at:
www.1stWorldLibrary.org/purchase.asp?ISBN=1-4218-2128-1

1st World Library Literary Society is a nonprofit
organization dedicated to promoting literacy by:

- Creating a free internet library accessible from any
computer worldwide.
- Hosting writing competitions and offering book
publishing scholarships.

Readers interested in supporting literacy
through sponsorship, donations or
membership please contact:
literacy@1stworldlibrary.org
Check us out at: www.1stworldlibrary.ORG
and start downloading free ebooks today.

The Banner Boy Scouts Afloat
contributed by Tim, Ed & Rodney
in support of
1st World Library Literary Society

CONTENTS

PREFACE

Dear Boys: -

It is with the greatest pleasure that I present you with the third volume of the "Banner Boy Scouts Series." This is a complete story in itself; and yet most of the leading characters you, who have already read the first and second volumes, will easily remember. I trust you will heartily welcome the appearance once more on the stage of Paul, Jack, Bobolink and all the other good fellows belonging to Stanhope Troop of Boy Scouts.

Those of you who are old friends will recollect that while the Red Fox Patrol was forming, the boys had a most strenuous time, what with a deep mystery in their midst, and the bitter strife resulting from their competition with rival troops belonging to neighboring towns. How the beautiful banner was cleverly won by Stanhope, I related in the first volume, called: "The Banner Boy Scouts."

In the succeeding story the Stanhope Scouts went on their first long hike, to camp in the open. The remarkable adventures they met with while enjoying this experience; as well as the stirring account of how they recovered a box of valuable papers that had been stolen from the office of Joe Clausin's father, form the main theme of "The Banner Boy Scouts on a Tour."

And now, in this third book, I have endeavored to interest you in another series of happenings that befell these wide-awake boys before their summer vacation was over. I hope you will, after reading this story through to the last line, agree with me that what the young assistant scout master, Paul Morrison, and his chums of Stanhope Troop endured while afloat all went to make them better and truer scouts in every sense of the word.

Cordially yours

GEORGE A. WARREN.

CHAPTER I

THE MYSTERIOUS BOXES

"What are you limping for, Bobolink?"

"Oh! shucks! I see there's no use trying to hide anything from your sharp eyes, Jack Stormways. Guess I just about walked my feet off today, goin' fishin' with our patrol leader, away over to the Radway River, and about six miles up."

"Have any luck, Bobolink?" instantly demanded the third member of the group of three half-grown boys, who were passing after nightfall through some of the partly deserted streets on the outskirts of the thriving town of Stanhope; and whose name it might be stated was Tom Betts.

"Well, I should say, yes. Between us we got seven fine bass, and a pickerel. By the way, I caught that pickerel; Paul, he looked after the bass end of the string, and like the bully chap he is divided with me;" and the boy who limped chuckled as he said this, showing that he could appreciate a joke, even when it was on himself.

About everybody in town called him Bobolink; and what boy could do otherwise, seeing that his real name was Robert O. Link?

As the trio of lads were all dressed in the khaki suits known all over the world nowadays as typifying Boy Scouts, it could be readily taken for granted that they belonged to the Stanhope Troop.

Already were there three full patrols enlisted, and wearing uniforms; while a fourth was in process of forming. The ones already in the field were known as, first, the Red Fox, to which these three lads belonged; then the Gray Fox, and finally the Black Fox. But as they had about exhausted the color roster of the fox family, the chances were that the next patrol would have to start on a new line when casting about for a name that would stamp their identity, and serve as a totem.

An efficient scout master had been secured in the person of a young man by the name of Mr. Gordon, who cheerfully accompanied the lads on their outings, and attended many of their meetings. But being a traveling salesman, Mr. Gordon often had to be away from home for weeks at a time.

When these lapses occurred, his duties fell upon the shoulders of Paul Morrison, who not only filled the position of leader to the Red Fox Patrol, but being a first-class scout, had received his commission from Headquarters that entitled him to act as assistant scout master to the whole troop during the absence of Mr. Gordon.

"How did you like it up on the Radway?" continued the one who had made the first inquiry, Jack Stormways, whose father owned a lumber yard and planing mill just outside the limits of the town, which was really the goal of their present after-supper walk.

"Great place, all right," replied Bobolink. "Paul kept calling my attention to all the things worth seeing. He seems to think a heap of the old Radway. For my part, I rather fancy our own tight little river, the Bushkill."

"Well, d'ye know, that's one reason I asked how you liked it," Jack went on. "Paul seemed so much taken with that region over there, I've begun to get a notion in my head he's fixing a big surprise, and that perhaps at the meeting to-night he may spring it on us."

"Tell me about that, will you?" exclaimed Bobolink, who was given to certain harmless slang ways whenever he became in the least excited, as at present. "Now that you've been and gone and given me a pointer, I c'n just begin to get a line on a few of the questions he asked me. Well, I'm willing to leave it to Paul. He always thinks of the whole shooting match when trying to give the troop a bully good time. Just remember what we went through with when we camped out up on Rattlesnake Mountain, will you?"

"That's right," declared Tom Betts, eagerly; "say, didn't we have the time of our lives, though?"

"And yet Paul said only today that as we had so long a time before vacation ends this year, a chance might pop up for another trip," Bobolink remarked, significantly.

"Did, eh? Well, don't that go to prove what I said; and you just wait till we get back to the meeting room in the church. Paul's just bursting with some sort of secret, and I reckon he'll just have to tell us to-night," and Jack laughed good-naturedly as he still led his two comrades on toward the retired lane, where his father's big mill adjoined the storage place for lumber; convenient to the river, and at the same time near the railroad, so that a spur track could enter the yard.

Besides these three boys five others constituted the Red Fox Patrol of Stanhope Troop. In the first story of this series, which appeared under the name of "The Banner Boy Scouts; Or, The Struggle for Leadership," the reader was told about the formation of the Red Fox Patrol, and how some of the boys learned a lesson in scout methods of returning good for evil; also how a cross old farmer was taught that he owed a duty to the community in which he lived, as well as to himself. In that story it was also disclosed how a resident of the town offered a beautiful banner to that troop which excelled in an open tournament also participated in by two other troops of Boy Scouts from the towns of Aldine and Manchester; the former on the east bank of the Bushkill, about six miles upstream, and the latter a bustling manufacturing place about seven miles down, and also on the same bank as Aldine.

In this competition, after a lively duel between the three wide awake troops, Stanhope won handsomely; and had therefore been given the banner, which Wallace Carberry proudly carried at the head of the procession whenever they paraded.

The second book, "The Banner Boy Scouts on a Tour; Or, The Mystery of Rattlesnake Mountain," was given over almost exclusively to descriptions of the wonderful things that came to pass when Stanhope Troop spent a part of their vacation camping out in order that those who were backward in their knowledge of how to take care of themselves when in the open should have a good chance to learn many of the secrets of Nature.

So many strange things happened to the boys when up on Rattlesnake Mountain that it would be utterly impossible to even mention them here; but if you wish to know all about the mystery they solved, and the numerous other exciting events that befell them, you must get the second volume.

There was to be a special meeting, which the acting scout master had called for this evening; and Bobolink, Jack, and Tom Betts expected to be back from their errand in time to answer to their names when the roll was called.

It was only to oblige Jack that the other two had left home half an hour earlier than was really necessary. Jack had asked them, over the telephone, to drop around, as he had to go out to his father's mill before he could attend the meeting in the church, where a room in the basement had been kindly loaned to them by the trustees.

"What's all this mean about you going to the mill at this queer old hour?" Bobolink was saying, as the three boys continued to walk on abreast, the speaker carrying the silver-plated bugle which he knew how to manipulate so well when the occasion allowed its use.

"Why, you see it's this way," Jack went on to explain. "My father knows a man of the name of Professor Hackett, though what he's a professor of you needn't ask me, because I don't know. But he's a bright little gentleman, all right; and somehow or other he looks like he's just cram full of some secret that's trying to break out all over him."

Bobolink laughed aloud.

"Well, that's a funny description you give of the gentleman, I must say, Jack; but go on - what's he got to do with our making this trip to the big mill tonight?"

"I just guess it's got everything to do with it," replied the other. "You see, the professor had a number of big cases sent up here on the train, and they came today, and were taken to the mill; for my father promised to keep them there a couple of days until the owner could take them away. What under the sun's in those big boxes I couldn't tell you from Adam; all I know is that he seems to be mighty much afraid somebody's going to steal them."

"Wow! and are we going there to stand guard over the blooming old things?" exclaimed Bobolink in dismay; for he would not want to miss that special meeting for anything.

"Oh! not quite so bad as that," answered Jack, with a laugh. "But you see, that professor wrote my father that he wanted him to hire a trusty man who would stay in the mill over night until he could get up here from New York and take the boxes away, somewhere or other."

"Oh, that's it, eh? And where do we find the guardian of the treasure? Is he going to bob up on the road to the mill?" Tom

Betts demanded.

"He promised father to be on deck at seven-thirty, and it'll be close on that by the time we get there, I reckon," Jack continued.

"And what have you got to do about it?" asked Bobolink.

"Let him in, and lock the door after he's on duty," replied Jack, promptly. "You see, ever since that attempt was made to burn the mill, when those hoboes, or yeggs, thought they'd find money in the safe, and had their trouble for their pains, my father has been mighty careful how he leaves the office unfastened. He couldn't see this man, Hans Waggoner, who used to work for us, but talked with him over the 'phone, and told him I'd be there to meet him, and let him in. That's all there is to it, boys, believe me."

"Only, you don't know what's in those boxes, and you'd give a cookie to find out?" suggested Bobolink.

"It isn't so bad as that," replied the other. "Of course I'm a little curious about what they might hold, that they have to be specially guarded; but I guess it's none of my business, and I'm not going to monkey around, trying to find out."

"Say, d'ye suppose your dad knows?" asked Tom.

"Sure he must," came from Jack, instantly. "He'd be silly to let anybody store a lot of cases that might hold dynamite, or any other old explosive, in his planing mill, without knowing all about 'em; wouldn't he? But my father don't think it's any of my affair, you see. And besides, I wouldn't be surprised if that funny little professor had bound him not to tell anybody about it. They got the boxes in on the sly, and that's a fact, boys."

"Oh! splash! now you've got me worked up with guessing, and I'll never be able to sleep till I know all about it," grumbled Bobolink.

"You're just as curious as any old woman I ever heard of," declared Jack.

"He always was," said Tom Betts, with a chuckle, "and I could string off more'n a few times when that same curiosity hauled Bobolink into a peck of trouble. But p'raps your father might let out the secret to you, after the old boxes have been taken away, and then you can ease his mind. Because it's just like he says, and he'll keep on dreamin' the most wonderful things about those cases you ever heard tell about. That imagination of Bobolink is something awful."

"Huh!" grunted the one under discussion, "not much worse than some others I know about right now; only they c'n keep a tight grip on theirs, and I'm that simple I just have to blurt everything out. Both of you fellers'd like to know nearly as much as I would, what that mysterious little old man has got hid away in those big cases. Of course you would. But you jump on the lid, and hold it down. It gets away with me; that's all."

"All the same, it's mighty good of you fellows, coming all the way out here with me tonight; and even when Bobolink's got a stone bruise on his heel, or something like that," Jack went on to say, with a vein of sincere affection in his voice; for the boys making up the Red Fox Patrol of Stanhope Troop were very fond of each other.

"Oh! rats! what's the good of being a scout if you can't do a comrade a little favor once in a while?" asked Bobolink, impetuously. "But there's the mill looming up ahead, Jack, in the dark. Half a moon don't give a whole lot of light, now, does it; and especially when it's a cloudy night in the bargain?"

"Well, I declare!" exclaimed Jack.

"What is it; did you see anything?" demanded Tom Betts, hastily.

"I'm not dead sure," admitted Jack; "you see, just as Bobolink said, the light's mighty poor, and a fellow could easily be mistaken; but I thought I saw something that looked like a tall man scuttle away around that corner of the mill, and dodge behind that pile of lumber!"

"Whew!" ejaculated Bobolink, showing the utmost interest, for excitement appealed to him.

"Say, perhaps Hans has arrived ahead of the half hour," suggested Tom Betts.

"No, it wasn't Hans, because I know him well, and he's a little runt of a Dutchman, but a fighter from the word go; and my father knows nobody's going to get away with those boxes of the professor while Hans and his musket, that was used in the Civil War, are on guard. That was a tall man, and he ran like he'd just heard us coming, and wanted to hide. I guess somebody else is curious about those boxes, besides Bobolink."

CHAPTER II

GLORIOUS NEWS

"Look! there he goes scooting away over past that other pile of lumber!" said Tom Betts, pointing as he spoke; and both the others caught a glimpse of a dim figure that was bending over while hurrying away, as if anxious not to be seen.

"Well, what d'ye think of the nerve of that?" ejaculated Bobolink, making a move as though in his impetuous way he was sorely tempted to chase after the disappearing figure of the unknown; only that the more cautious Jack threw out a hand, and caught hold of his sleeve.

"Never mind him, boys," remarked the son of the lumber man. "Perhaps it was only a tramp from the railroad, after all, meaning to find a place to sleep among the lumber piles. But I'm going to tell my father about it, all the same. Seems to me he ought to have some one like Hans stay here every night. Some of those hoboes will set fire to things, either by accident, or because they are mad at the town for not handing enough good things out to suit their appetites."

They walked on, and in another minute were at the office door. There they sat down on the stoop to rest and talk; but only a few minutes had passed when they heard the sound of approaching footsteps; and a small but very erect figure appeared, carrying an old-fashioned musket of the vintage of '61 over his shoulder.

"Hello! Hans, on time all right, I see!" called out Jack.

"Dot is me, I dells you, every time. I am punctuality idself. I sets me der clock, undt figure dot all oudt, so I haf yust der time to valk here. Der sooner you obens der door, Misder Jack, der sooner I pe on der chob," was the reply of the little man who had been hired to watch the mill, and those strange boxes, during the night.

Evidently Hans was "strictly business." He had been hired to watch, and he wanted to be earning his wages as quickly as possible.

So Jack used his key, and the four entered the office. It was quite a good-sized room. The windows were covered with heavy wire netting, and it seemed strong enough to resist any ordinary degree of force. After that attempt to rob his safe, Mr. Stormways had taken precautions against a similar raid.

The watchman also carried a lantern, which he now lighted. No sooner had this been done than Bobolink uttered an exclamation.

"I reckon now, Jack, that these three big boxes are the ones the professor wants watched?" he observed, pointing as he spoke to several cumbersome cases that stood in a group, occupying considerable space.

Tom Betts, also looking, saw that they were unusually well fastened. In addition to the ordinary nailing, they were bound along the edges with heavy twisted wire, through which frequent nails had been driven. When they came to be opened, the job would prove no easy one.

"Yes, those are the ones; and Hans is to spend most all his time right here in the office," Jack went on to say. "I'm going to ask my father if he ought not to hire you to be night watchman right along, Hans. This plant of ours is getting too big a thing to leave unguarded, with so many tramps coming along the road in the good old summer time. I suppose you'd like the job, all right?"

"Sure," replied the bustling little man, his eyes sparkling. "I always did enchoy vorkin' for Misder Stormways. Undt it habbens dot yust now I am oudt off a chob. Dot vill pe allright. I hopes me idt turns out so. Undt now, off you like, you could lock der door some. I stay me here till somepody gomes der mornin' py."

"Oh! you keep the key, Hans," replied Jack. "You might want to chase out after some one; but father told me to warn you not to be tempted to go far away. You see, he's storing these cases for a friend, and it seems that somebody wants to either get at 'em, or steal them. They're what you're hired to protect, Hans. And now let us out, and lock the door after we're gone."

Anxious to get to the church before the meeting could be called to order, the three scouts did not linger, although Hans was such an amusing little man that they would have liked nothing better than to spend an hour in his society, listening to stories about his adventures - for the Dutchman had roamed pretty much all over the world since his boyhood.

"Shucks! I forgot to examine those boxes," lamented Bobolink, when they were on the way past the end of the lumber yard.

Jack was glancing sharply about, wondering whether that tall, skulking figure they had glimpsed could be some one who had a peculiar interest in the boxes stored in the office of the mill until Professor Hackett called for them; or just an ordinary "Weary Willie," looking for a soft board to sleep on, before he continued his hike along the railroad track.

But look as he would, he could see no further sign of a trespasser. Of course that was no sign the unknown might not be within twenty feet of them, right then. The tall piles of lumber offered splendid hiding-places if any one was disposed to take advantages of the nooks; Jack had explored many a snug hole, when roaming through the yard at various times, and ought to know about it.

"Oh! I took care of that part," chuckled Tom Betts. "I saw you were talking with Jack and old Hans, so I just stepped up, and walked around the boxes. There isn't a thing on 'em but the name of the professor, and Jack's dad's address in Stanhope."

"And they didn't look much like animal cages to me," muttered Bobolink; upon which both of the others emitted exclamations of surprise, whereupon the speaker seemed to think he ought to make some sort of explanation, so he went on hastily: "You see, Jack, I somehow got a silly idea in my mind that p'raps this little professor was some sort of an animal trainer, and meant to come up here, just to have things quiet while he did his little stunts. But that was a punk notion for me, all right; there ain't any smell of animals about those boxes, not a whiff."

"But what in the wide world gave you that queer notion?" asked Tom.

"Don't know," replied Bobolink, "'less it was what Jack said about the professor writing up from Coney Island near New York City; that's the place where all the freaks show every summer. I've been down there myself."

"Listen to him, would you, Jack, owning up that he's a sure enough freak? Well, some of us had a little idea that way, Bobolink, but we never thought you'd admit it so coolly," remarked Tom Betts, laughingly.

"And the wild animal show down there is just immense," the other went on, not heeding the slur cast upon his reputation; for like many boys, Bobolink had a pretty tough skin, and was not easily offended; "and I guess I've thought about what I saw done there heaps of times. So Coney stands for wild animal trainin' to me. But that guess was away wide of the mark. Forget it, fellows. Only whenever Jack here learns what was in those boxes, he must let his chums know. It's little enough to pay for draggin' a lame scout all the way out here tonight; think so, Jack?"

"I sure do, and you'll have it, if ever I find out," was the reply. "Perhaps, after they've been taken away by the professor, my father mightn't mind telling me what was in them. And we'll let it rest at that, now."

"But you mark me, if Bobolink gets any peace of mind till he learns," warned Tom.

Chatting on various matters connected more or less with the doings of the Boy Scout movement, and what a fine thing it was proving for the youth of the whole land, Jack and his chums presently brought up at the church which had the bell tower; and where a splendid meeting room had been given over for their occupancy in the basement, in which a gymnasium was fitted up for use in the fall and winter.

In that tower hung a big bell, whose brazen tongue had once upon a time alarmed the good people of Stanhope by ding-donging at a most unusual hour. It had come through a prank played upon the scouts by several tough boys of the town whose enmity Paul Morrison and his chums had been unfortunate enough to incur. But for the details of that exciting episode the reader will have to be referred back to the preceding volume.

Jack Stormways never glanced up at that tower but that he was forcibly reminded of that startling adventure; and a smile would creep over his face as he remembered some of the most striking features connected with the event.

In the big room the three scouts found quite a crowd awaiting their coming. Indeed, it seemed as though nearly every member of the troop had made it an especial point to attend this meeting just as though they knew there was something unusual about to come before them for consideration.

As many of these lads will be apt to figure in the pages of this story, it might be just as well to listen to the secretary, as he calls the roster of the Stanhope Troop. Once this duty had devolved upon one of the original Red Fox Patrol; but with the idea of sharing the responsibilities in a more general way, it had been transferred to the shoulders of Phil Towns, who belonged to the second patrol.

RED FOX PATROL

1 - Paul Morrison, patrol leader, and also assistant scout master.
2 - Jack Stormways.
3 - Bobolink, the official bugler.
4 - Bluff Shipley, the drummer.
5 - Nuthin, whose real name was Albert Cypher.
6 - William Carberry, one of the twins.
7 - Wallace Carberry, the other.
8 - Tom Betts.

GRAY FOX PATROL

1 - Jud Elderkin, patrol leader.
2 - Joe Clausin.
3 - Andy Flinn.
4 - Phil Towns.
5 - Horace Poole.
6 - Bob Tice.
7 - Curly Baxter.
8 - Cliff Jones, whose entire name was Clifford Ellsworth Fairfax Jones.

BLACK FOX PATROL

1 - Frank Savage, patrol leader.
2 - Billie Little, a very tall lad, and of course always called Little Billie.
3 - Nat Smith.
4 - Sandy Griggs.

5 - Old Dan Tucker.
6 - "Red" Conklin.
7 - "Spider" Sexton.
8 - "Gusty" Bellows.

Unattached, but to belong to a fourth patrol, later on:

George Hurst.
"Lub" Ketcham.

Thus it will be seen that there were now twenty-six lads connected with the wide awake Stanhope Troop, and more coming.

After the roll call, they proceeded to the regular business, with Paul Morrison in the chair, he being the president of the association. It was surprising how well many of these boyish meetings were conducted; Paul and some of his comrades knew considerable about parliamentary law, and long ago the hilarious members of the troop had learned that when once the meeting was called to order they must put all joking aside.

Many a good debate had been heard within those same walls since the scouts received permission to meet there; and yet in camp, when the rigid discipline was relaxed, these same fellows could be as full of fun and frolic as any lads going.

Tonight it had been whispered around that Paul had some sort of important communication to make. No one could give a guess as to what it might be, although all sorts of hazards were attempted, only to be jeered at as absurd.

And so, while the meeting progressed, they were growing more and more excited, until finally it was as much as some of them could do to repress a cheer when Paul, having made sure that there was no other business to be transacted, arose with a smile, and announced that he had a certain communication to lay before them.

"Are you ready to hear it?" he asked; "every fellow who is raise his hand."

Needless to say, not a single hand remained unraised. Paul deliberately counted them to the bitter end.

"Just twenty-four; and as that is the total number present, we'll call it unanimous," he said, just to tantalize them a little; and then, with an air of business he went on: "Two splendid gentlemen of this town, by name Mr. Everett and Colonel Bliss, happen to own motorboats. As they have gone to Europe, to be away until late in the Fall, they thought it would show how they appreciated the work of the Stanhope Troop of Boy Scouts if they offered the free use of their two boats to us, to make a cruise wherever we thought best during the balance of vacation time. Now, all in favor of accepting this magnificent offer from our fellow townsmen signify by saying 'aye!'"

Hardly had the words fallen from the speaker's lips when a thunderous "aye" made the stout walls of the building tremble.

CHAPTER III

FOR CEDAR ISLAND - GHOST OR NO GHOST

"Three cheers for Colonel Bliss and Mr. Everett!" called out Bobolink, almost too excited to speak plainly.

Paul himself led the cheering, because he knew those delighted boys just had to find some sort of outlet for the enthusiasm that was bubbling up within them. And doubtless the walls of that sacred building had seldom heard such cheers since away back in the time when a meeting was held there at news of the Civil War breaking out in 1861 and the patriotic citizens had formed a company on the spot, to volunteer their services to the President.

"Where will we go?" called out one scout, after the cheering had died down, and they found time to consider ways and means of employing the motorboats that had been so generously given into their keeping.

"Down the Bushkill to the sea!" suggested one.

"I suppose you think these motorboats can jump like broncos?" declared Jud Elderkin, with a look of disgust; "else how would they ever get around that big dam down at Seely's Mills? We could crawl a few miles *up* the Bushkill, but to go down would mean only a short cruise."

"Let Paul say!" cried Bobolink, shrewdly reading the smile on the face of the assistant scout master, as he listened to all sorts of wild plans, none of which would hold together when the rest of the scouts started to pick flaws.

"Yes, Paul's got a scheme that'll knock all these wildcat ones just to flinders, see if it don't," remarked Tom Betts, waving his hands to enforce silence.

"Go on and tell us, Paul; and I reckon I c'n give a right smart guess that it's about that Radway River country," declared Bobolink.

"Just what it is," said Paul. "Listen, then, and tell me what you think of my plan. I've figured it all out, and believe we could make it a go. If we did, we'd surely have the time of our lives, and find out something that I've wanted myself to know a long while back. It's about a trip up the Radway River, too, just as our smart chum guessed."

"But, say, the boats are right here at Stanhope, and have been used in running up and down the Bushkill; then how in the name of wonder can we carry them over to the Radway, which is some miles away, I take it?" asked William Carberry, soberly.

"Wait and see; Paul's got all that arranged," declared the confident Tom Betts.

"Have 'em hauled over on one of his father's big lumber wagons, mebbe," suggested Nuthin, who was rather a small chap, though not of quite so little importance as his name would seem to indicate.

"Oh, you make me tired, Nuthin," declared Bobolink; "why, those motorboats weigh a ton or two apiece. Think of gettin' a wagon strong enough to carry one; and all the slow trips it'd have to take to get 'em there and back. I reckon the whole of our vacation'd see us on the dry land part of the cruise. Now, let Paul tell us what plan he's been thinking about to get over to the Radway with 'em."

"Well, it's just this way," the chairman of the meeting went on to say, calmly, with the air of one who had studied the matter carefully, and grasped every little detail; "most of you know that there was a stream known as Jackson Creek that ran into the Bushkill a mile below Manchester. That was once dredged out, and made to form a regular canal connecting the two rivers. For years, my father says, it was used regularly by all sorts of boats that wanted to cross over from one river to the other. But changes came, and by degrees the old canal has been about forgotten. Still, it's there; and I went through it in my canoe just yesterday, to sound, and see if it could be used by the motorboats now."

"And could it?" asked Bobolink, eagerly.

"I think there's a fair chance that we'd pull through, though it might sometimes be a close shave. There's a lot of nasty mud in the canal, because, you see, it hasn't been cleaned out for years. If we had a good rain now, and both rivers raised, we wouldn't have any trouble, but could run through easy enough."

"Well, supposing we did get through, how far up the Radway would we push?" asked Bobolink, determined to get the entire proposition out of Paul at once, now that they had him going.

"All the way to Lake Tokala," replied Paul, promptly. "Some of you happen to know that there's a jolly island in that big lake, known as Cedar Island, because right on top of a small hill in the middle, a splendid cedar stands. Well, we could take our tents along, and make camp on that island, fishing, swimming, and having one of the best times ever heard of. What do you say, fellows?"

Immediately there was a clamor of tongues. Some seemed to be for accepting Paul's suggestion with a whoop, and declared that it took them by storm. A few, however, seemed to raise objections; and such was the racket that nobody was able to make himself understood. So the chairman called for order;

and with the whack of his gavel on the table every voice was stilled.

"Let's conduct this meeting in a parliamentary way," said Paul. "Some of you must have thought it stood adjourned. Now, whoever wants to speak, get up, and let's hear what you've got to say."

"I move that we take up the plan offered, and make our headquarters on Cedar Island," said Wallace Carberry, rising.

"Not on your life!" declared Curly Baxter, bobbing up like a jack-in-the-box; "I've heard lots about that same place. It's troubled with a *mystery*, and only last week I heard Paddy Reilly say he'd never go there fishin' again if he was paid for it. He's dreadfully afraid of ghosts, Paddy is."

"Ghosts!" almost shouted William Carberry; "I vote to go to Cedar Island then. I've always wanted to see a genuine ghost, and never yet had a chance."

"Now, I heard that it was a wild man that lived somewhere on that same island," remarked Frank Savage. "They say he's a terror, too, all covered with hair; and one man who'd been looking for pearl mussels in the river up that way told my father he beat any Wild Man of Borneo he'd ever set eyes on in a freak show or circus."

"Oh, that's a fine place for honest scouts to pitch their tents, ain't it - I don't think!" observed Joe Clausin, with a sneer.

"H-h-huh! ain't there j-j-just twenty-six of us s-s-scouts; and ought we b-b-be afraid of one l-l-little g-g-ghost, or even a w-w-wild man?" demanded Bluff Shipley, who stuttered once in a while, when unduly excited, though he was by degrees overcoming the nervous habit.

"Put it to a vote, Mr. Chairman!" called out Bobolink.

"Yes, and majority rules, remember," warned William Carberry.

"But that don't mean a feller just *has* to go along, does it?" asked Nuthin, looking somewhat aghast at the thought.

"Of course it don't;" Bobolink told him; "all the same you'll be on deck, my boy. I just know you can't resist having such a jolly good time, ghost or not. Question, Mr. Chairman!"

"Vote! Vote!"

"All in favor of trying to go through the old canal that used to connect the Bushkill with the Radway, and cruising up to Cedar Island, camping there for a week or ten days, say 'aye,'" Paul went on to remark.

A thunderous response cheered his heart; for somehow Paul seemed very much set upon following out the scheme he himself had devised.

"Contrary, no!" he continued.

There were just three who boldly allowed themselves to be set down as not being in favor of the daring plan - Nuthin, Curly Baxter and Joe Clausin; and yet, just as the wise, far-seeing Bobolink had declared, when it came to a question of staying at home while the rest of the troop were off enjoying their vacation, or swallowing their fear of ghosts and wild men, these three boys would be along when the motorboats started on their adventurous cruise.

"The ayes have it; and the meeting stands adjourned, according to the motion I can see Jack Stormways's just about to put," and with a laugh Paul stepped down from the platform.

For fully half an hour they talked the thing over. It was viewed from every possible angle. Many objections raised by the doubters were promptly met by the ready Paul; and in the end it was definitely decided that they would give just one day to making all needed preparations.

They had tents for the three patrols now, and all sorts of cooking utensils; for frequently the scouts were divided into messes, there being a cook appointed in each patrol.

What was needed most of all were the supplies for an extended stay; and when it was taken into consideration that a score of boys, with ravenous appetites, would want three big meals each and every day, the question of figuring out enough provisions to see them through was no light matter.

But then they had considerable money in the treasury, and a numbers of the boys said they would bring loaves of bread, and all sorts of eatables from home; so Paul saw his way clear toward providing the given quantity.

"Don't forget that the gasoline is going to eat a big hole into our little pile of the long green," remarked Curly Baxter, still engaged in trying to throw cold water on the scheme.

"Oh, that makes me think of something I forgot to tell you, fellows," declared Paul, his face filled with good humor. "One of the stipulations connected with the lending of these two motor-boats by the kind gentlemen who own them was that they insisted on supplying all the liquid fuel needed to run the craft. The tanks are to be filled, and each boat carries in addition another drum, with extra gasoline. We'll likely have enough for all our needs that way, and without costing us a red cent, either. So, you see how easy most of your objections melt away, Curly. Chances are, you'll fall into line, and be with us when we start the day after tomorrow."

Several of the boys were feeling pretty blue. They wanted to accompany the rest of the troop the worst way; but it happened that their folks had planned to go down to the sea-shore for a month, until school began again; and the chances were they would have to go along, though every one of them declared they would choose the cruise up the Radway in the two motorboats, if given their way.

But it looked as though there was going to be a pretty fair crowd on each boat. Paul counted noses of those he believed would be along, and found that they seemed to number eighteen. If two of the three timid ones concluded to throw their fears to the winds, and come along, it would make an even twenty.

"Of course, it will be hard to sleep so many aboard, because the boats are small affairs, taken altogether," Paul observed; "but we hope to make the journey in a full day, and be on Cedar Island by nightfall."

"Whew! night on Cedar Island - excuse *me* if you please!" faltered Curly Baxter, holding up both hands, as though the idea suggested all sorts of terrible things to his mind; but much as he seemed desirous of causing others to back out, Paul saw no signs of any one doing so.

"Meet here at noon tomorrow, boys, and I'll report what I've done. Then we can figure on what else we have to lay in store, so as to be comfortable. We must get everything down to the boats before evening, because we start early on Wednesday, you hear. At eight A. M., Bobolink, here, will sound his bugle; and ten minutes later we weigh anchor, or cut loose our hawsers, as you choose to say it, for it means letting go a rope after all."

They started home in bunches, as usual, those who happened to live near together naturally waiting for each other. Paul, Jack, and Bobolink walked together.

"And just as it happens so many times," Paul was saying, as they sauntered on in the direction of home. "Mr. Gordon is away on the road somewhere, selling goods; so we have to go without having our fine scoutmaster along to look after us."

"Guess nobody will miss him very much, although Mr. Gordon is a mighty nice man and we all think a heap of him; but you are able to fill his shoes all right, Paul; and, somehow, it seems to feel better not to have any grown-up along. The responsibility makes most of the fellers behave, and think for themselves, you see," Jack went on to say.

Paul heaved a little sigh, for he knew who shouldered most of that same responsibility.

"But," remarked Bobolink, as he was about to separate from Jack and Paul on a certain corner, where their ways divided; "I'd give something right now to just know what's in those queer old boxes Professor Hackett has stored in your mill, Jack; and why they have to be watched, just like they held money or something that has to be guarded against an unknown enemy! But I guess I'll have to take it out in wantin', because you don't know, and wouldn't tell till you got the consent of your dad, even if you did. Goodnight, fellows; and here's hoping we're going to have the time of our lives up and around Cedar Island!"

CHAPTER IV

LAYING IN THE STORES

Well, it was a busy day for the scouts of Stanhope Troop.

There was the greatest running back and forth, and consultations among the lads, ever known. Where a parent seemed doubtful about giving permission for a boy to take part in the intended cruise, influence was brought to bear on coaxing neighbors to drop in, and tell how glad they were their boys were independent, as it was the finest thing that could ever come to them; and also what slight chances there seemed to be of any accident happening that might not occur when the lads stayed at home, where they would go in swimming anyhow.

And owing to the masterly way in which the objections of certain parents were met and overcome, long before noon every boy who had a ghost of a chance of sailing on the two motor-boats reported that he had gained consent; even Curly Baxter admitted that his folks had been won over, and that he "could go along, if so he he chose to shut his eyes to facts, and just trust to luck," which, be it said, he finally did, just as Paul had believed would be the case.

Meanwhile Paul and Jack were making their purchases of provisions, using a list that had been found useful on their other camping trip; although several little inaccuracies were corrected. For instance, they had taken too much rice on that other occasion; and not enough ham, and salt pork, and breakfast bacon.

Eggs they hoped to buy from some farmer over on the mainland; and possibly milk as well. Jack even hinted that they might feel disposed, if the money held out, to get a few chickens, and have one grand feed before breaking camp.

"And this time we'll try and make sure that none of our grub is hooked, like it was when we camped up on old Rattlesnake Mountain," Jack had declared, with emphasis, for the memory of certain mysterious things that had happened to them on that occasion often arose to disturb some of the scouts.

"Oh! it ought to be easy to look out for that part of the job," Paul had made answer; "because, you see, we'll have the two boats to store things in, and they can be anchored out in the lake, if we want, each with a guard aboard."

By noon the whole town knew all about the expected cruise. Boys who did not have the good luck to belong to Stanhope Troop became greatly excited over it; and by their actions and looks showed how envious they were of their schoolmates.

Just about then, if the assistant scout master had called for volunteers, he could have filled two complete additional patrols with candidates; for the fellows began to realize that the scouts were having three times as much fun as any one else.

But Paul was too wise for that. He believed in selecting the right sort of boys, and not taking every one who offered his name, just because he wanted to have a good time. These fellows would not be able to live up to the iron-clad rules that scouts have got to subscribe to, and which are pretty much covered in the twelve cardinal principles which, each boy declares in the beginning, he will try and govern his life by - "to be trustworthy, loyal, helpful, friendly, courteous, kind, obedient, cheerful, thrifty, brave, clean, and reverent."

Some of the scouts were at Headquarters, as the room under the church was called, getting the supplies there in order, to take down to the boats later on, when they were surprised to have a visitor in the shape of old Peleg Growdy.

This man lived just outside the town limits, on the main road. He had once kept his wagon yard in a very disgraceful condition, much to the disgust of the women folks of Stanhope. The boys, too, looked upon Peleg as a crusty old fellow, who hated their kind.

He had done something to offend one of the scouts, and it was proposed that they play some sort of trick on the old fellow in order to pay him back; but Paul ventured to say that if the scouts went in a body to his place, when he was asleep, and cleaned up his wagon yard so that it looked neat, he would have his eyes opened to the debt he owed the community.

Paul, it seemed, had learned the main cause of the old man's holding aloof from his neighbors. It came from the fact that some years back he had lost his wife and children in the burning of his house; and ever since had looked upon boys as especially created to worry lone widowers who wanted only to be let alone.

Well, the scouts certainly made a great friend of Peleg Growdy. He had even tried to induce them to let him purchase their suits to show that he was a changed man; but of course they could not allow that, because each true scout must earn every cent of the money with which his outfit in the beginning is bought. But in many ways had old Peleg shown them that he was now going to be one of the best friends the boys of Stanhope Troop had ever possessed.

He had heard about their intended trip, when he came to town with some produce; and rather than go back home with some things for which there did not seem to be any sale at the price he wanted, he had come around with his wagon to ask his boy friends to please him by accepting them as his contribution to the cause.

They could not disappoint the generous-hearted old man by refusing; and besides the half-bushel of onions, and double the quantity of new potatoes, looked mighty fine to the lads.

About two o'clock, when it seemed that their list was about complete, even though they would doubtless think of a lot of things after it was too late to get them, Paul decided to send for the wagon that was to haul the tents and other things, including blankets for the crowd, brought from various homes to the meeting place, down to the waiting boats.

"I wanted to get Ezra Sexton, but he was busy," Jack explained, when he had carried out the errand given into his charge; "fact is, I hear, Bobolink, that Ezra came early this morning with an order from the professor, and took all those big cases away in his two wagons."

"Well, that was quick work now, wasn't it?" grumbled Bobolink; "reckon I won't ever have a chance to see what was inside those boxes. Say, see here, d'ye happen to know where Ezra hauled 'em? Not to the railroad, I should think, because they only came that way yesterday."

But Jack shook his head.

"Some distance off, I reckon, because the trucks don't seem to be back yet, so I couldn't get to see Ezra," he remarked; "but when we come home again, I'll ask my father about it, and relieve that curiosity of yours, Bobolink."

"Huh! that means mebbe two weeks or so I'm to go on guessing, I s'pose," the other remarked, in a disconsolate way that made Jack laugh.

"Funny how you do get a notion in that coco of yours; and it'd take a crowbar to work it loose," he observed, at which the other only grinned, saying:

"Born that way; must 'a made a mistake and left the wrong article at our house for the new baby; thought it was a girl; always wantin' to know everything, and never happy till I get it. But Jack, I'll try and keep this matter out of my mind. Don't pay any attention to me, if I look cross once in a while. That'll be when it's got me gripped fast, and I'm tryin' to guess."

"I've known you to do the same when you had one of those puzzles, trying to work it," chuckled Jack Stormways. "Fact is, I remember that once you told me you sat up till two o'clock in the morning over that ring business."

"But I got her, Jack - remember that; won't you? If I hadn't I'd been burning the midnight oil yet, I reckon. 'Taint safe to make *me* a present of a puzzle, because I'm just dead sure to nearly split my poor weak brain trying to figger it out. And Jack, I'll never be happy till I know what was in those boxes; and why did that sly little professor believe someone wanted to steal his thunder and lightning?"

It took several loads to carry all their traps down to the boats. But finally, as the groceries had also been delivered, the scouts took count of their stock, and it was believed they had about everything, save what the boys might bring in the morning from home.

Paul advised them to go slow with regard to what they carried along, as they did not expect to be gone six months. If any garments gave out, why, there would be plenty of soap and water handy; and the fellow who did not know how to wash a pair of socks, or some handkerchiefs, had better take a few lessons on how to play laundry woman in an emergency.

"If things keep on multiplying much more," the scout master remarked, as he looked around at the tremendous amount of stuff which the boys were now beginning to stow away systematically; "why we won't be able to navigate the boats through that shallow canal at all. They'll just stick fast, because they'll be so low down in the water; and chances are we'll have to spend all our vacation slobbering around in that mud trying to coax them along. Go slow, fellows; bring just as little as you possibly can in the morning. If there's any doubt about it being a real necessity, why leave it at home. We're all scouts and true comrades, ready to share and share alike; so, no matter what happens, no one will go without."

Of course there were many persons who came down to watch the loading of the supplies, for half of Stanhope was interested in the expedition; and groups of envious boys could be seen in various nooks, taking note of all that went on, while they wished they had such good luck.

No one was allowed on board who had no business there. Of course when any of the fathers or mothers of the boys who were going happened along, they were only too proudly shown through both boats, and had everything explained by half a dozen eager scouts. But a couple of guards stood at the gangplank, and no boy was allowed aboard unless accompanied by his parents; and even then a strict watch was kept, because there were some pretty mean fellows in town, who believed in the motto of "rule or ruin." When they were not allowed to play, they always tried their best to see to it that no one else played, either.

"There's Ted Slavin and Ward Kenwood sitting up on the bank over there, Paul," remarked Jack, about half an hour before the time when the scouts would have to be going home to their suppers.

"I've been watching them," replied the scout master; "and from the way they carry on, laughing when they put their heads together, I had just about made up my mind that they were hatching up some mischief."

"Mischief!" echoed Bobolink, who was close by at the moment, and heard what was being said; "say, that's too nice a word to use when talking about the pranks of that combination. Ward, he supplies some of the brains, and all of the hard plunks; while that bully, Ted Slavin, does the work, or gets some of his cronies to do it for him. Now, I wonder if they'll try to come aboard here, and play hob with our stuff, like they did once before when we were all ready to hike off on a jaunt?"

"Don't bother yourself about that, Bobolink," said Paul, quietly. "I had decided, even before I noticed Ward and Ted, that we must have a guard stay on board all night. I'm going to see right now what fellows can be spared. They can go home to supper, and some of us will wait for them to come back."

"Let me be one, Paul; won't you?" pleaded Bobolink.

"But you are so quick to act, and it might bring on trouble," objected the other.

"Oh! I'll promise to think five times before I act once; and besides, there'll be some fellow along, like Jack here, who can keep me quiet. Of course, though, if you believe I'm not fit to do the work, why -"

"That'll do for you, Bobolink," Paul broke in, "if your folks say you can stay, come back ready to camp on board. I'll find you one or two mates - four if possible - so you can sleep in relays of twos. And I'll also try to fix up some dodge that will cool those fellows off, in case they try to jump aboard between sunset and daylight."

"Huh! I'd rather *warm* their jackets for 'em," growled Bobolink; who, having suffered before at the hands of the meanest boy in Stanhope, Ted Slavin, had only the poorest opinion of him, and of those who trained in his company.

"When I come back tonight, after supper," continued Paul, "I'm going to fetch my shotgun along. It might come in handy on the cruise in case we ran up against a wildcat, or something like that. And I've known such a thing as a double-barrel to be mighty useful, when fired in the air, to make sneaking boys nearly jump out of their skins with alarm - but always in the air, remember, Bobolink."

"Oh! don't worry about me; my bite is not half as bad as my bark. I like to make out I'm just fierce, when all the while, if you could look inside, you'd find me chuckling to beat the band. I wouldn't shoot a gun at anybody, unless it was to save another fellow's life; and then I'd try to pepper his legs. Fetch the gun, Paul; it'll come in real handy."

So, when Paul did come back after dark, he carried the weapon under his arm in true hunter style; for Paul had been several times up in Maine, and knew a good deal of woodcraft, having had actual experience, which is better than theory, any day.

These four scouts were left in charge of the two boats, when finally Paul went back home to get some sleep before the eventful day that was to witness the sailing of the motorboat expedition:

Bobolink; Tom Betts; Spider Sexton, of the Black Fox Patrol and Andy Flinn, who belonged to the Gray Foxes; and firmly did they promise Paul to keep a bright lookout to make sure that no harm came to the boats during the long night.

CHAPTER V

JUST AFTER THE CLOCK STRUCK TEN

"Here we are, monarchs of all we survey," remarked Bobolink, as the last of the other scouts went off, leaving the four guards to their task of taking care of those two fine motorboats for the night.

It was nine o'clock.

The well-known sounds from the church steeple had told them that; and somehow every fellow counted the strokes aloud, as though on this night in particular they meant far more than at other times.

Stanhope, not being a manufacturing town, like Manchester, was, as a rule, rather quiet of nights; except when the Glorious Fourth was being celebrated; or some other holiday kept the younger element on the move.

Bobolink had been given the post of "Captain of the Guards;" while Tom Betts was to be considered the second in command. They were to divide the duties in such fashion that there would be two of them on deck at a time.

"I'll take Andy for my mate; and you can have Spider to help out," Bobolink had told Tom, when they were arranging the programme.

"And how long will the watches be?" demanded Spider, who liked to sleep about as much as any fellow in the troop; he had gained that odd name not because he was artful and cruel; but on account of his slender legs, which long ago some smart boy had likened to those of a spider; and it only requires a hint like that to establish a nick-name.

"Two hours each, divided into four," replied the chief, feeling the responsibility of his position; for this was really the first time Bobolink could remember being placed over any of his fellow scouts - Paul wished to "try him out," and discover what sort of reliance could be placed in the lad.

"That's an awful short time to get a snooze," complained Spider, yawning. "Why, you'd hardly get asleep before you'd have to wake up."

"Then what's the use going to sleep at all, at all?" remarked Andy Flinn, with a broad smile. "Let's draw lots to say who'll stand guard the whole night"

"Well, I guess not," objected Spider, vigorously. "Half a loaf is some better'n no bread, they always say; and four hours ought to make a fellow feel as though he hadn't been shut out altogether from his needed rest."

"Needed rest is good for you, Spider; the only trouble is you need too much," Bobolink remarked. "But here's the way we'll fix it: Andy and me, why, we'll be the pioneers on the job, starting in right now, while you others curl up somewhere, and get busy taking your forty winks. At eleven-ten we'll give you the foot, and take your places. Jack left me his little watch, so we could tell how time goes; but sure, you can hear the clock in the church steeple knock off the hours. And for the last time, listen to me; not one wink must any sentry take while on duty. Sleeping on post is the most terrible thing you can do. They shoot soldiers in war time who betray their trust that way. Get your instructions, fellows?"

"I'm on to what you mean, all right," said Spider; "and I guess I know my weakness, as well as anybody. To prove that I want to do the right thing, I'm going to fix it up with my mate to give me a jab with this pin, every time he gets a notion in his head that I'm drowsing."

"Say, that sounds heroic all right," remarked Bobolink, doubtfully; "but you don't want to get too gay with that same pin, Tom. It'd be a shame to wake Andy and me up every ten minutes, making Spider give a yelp. Better just shake him if he acts sleepy. And above everything else, keep a bright watch along the shore."

"Think they'll be apt to come from that direction, do you?" asked Spider.

"Just as like as not," the other returned; "but that isn't saying you ought not to keep an eye on the other side, and all around. I wouldn't put it past that Ted Slavin to swim down this way from some place above, thinking he could do his little trick by fooling us, and coming aboard on the water side."

"Whew! do you really think, then, he'd dare board these boats, knowing that they belong to two of the richest and most prominent citizens of Stanhope?" asked Spider, who occasionally liked to air his command of fine language.

"Well, you ought to be on to the curves of that Ted Slavin; and if you just look back to things he's been known to do in the past, why, lots of times he's played his pranks on people that had a pull. Why, didn't he even sneak into the loft over Police Headquarters once, and rig up a scare that came near breaking up the force. Ted fixed it so the wind'd work through a knot-hole in the dark, whenever he chose to pull a string over the fence back of the house, and make the awfullest groaning noise anybody ever did hear. It got on the nerves of Chief Billings and his men. They hunted that loft over and over, but of course the groans didn't come when they were up there. Why, he had 'em so badly rattled that they all just about camped out on the pavement the rest of that night."

"Sure, I remember that," declared Andy Flinn, laughing. "Three nights did he play the same joke, and then they got on to him. Wan officer do be sneakin' up to the loft, while the rist pretended to be huntin' around downstairs. He discovered the sthring, cript downstairs again, wint out on the sly, and, be the powers, followed it to the fince. Then he wint around, and jumped on Tid while the bhoy was a pullin' his sthring like smoke, makin' worse groanings than any time yit. Sure they thried to hush the joke up, the police was that ashamed; but it cript out some way."

"Well, get off to bed, Spider and Tom;" said Bobolink, "we'll wake you up when it's time to change the watch. And remember what a nice little surprise we've got ready for anybody who thinks he can meddle with things that don't belong to him. Skip out now, both of you."

The two motorboats had been lashed side by side. They were about of a size, and something like twenty-four feet in length, with a rather generous beam, because their owners went in for pleasure and comfort, rather than racing. Still, one of the boats, the *Speedwell*, was said to be capable of doing a mile in seven minutes, if pushed, on flat water; while the other, called the *Comfort*, being broader, could not do anything like that.

It was easy to pass from one boat to the other, as they lay there. Each had a canopy top, and curtains that could be dropped, and buttoned, during a wet spell, or if the owner chose to sleep aboard; but on this occasion Paul had believed it best that these latter should remain up, so as to allow of free observation all around.

A stout hawser secured the boat nearest the shore to a big stake that had been driven deeply into the earth. Thus the boats lay close beside a short dock that was called a landing stage. As the current of the Bushkill was always pretty strong there must be more or less of a strain on that hawser; but since it was comparatively new, the boys felt that there could not be the slightest danger of its breaking, unless some outside influence were brought to bear on it, such as a keen-edged knife blade.

In that case, as it was very taut, it would naturally part readily; and with consequences disastrous to the safety of the two boats, which must be carried off down-stream in the darkness, possibly to be driven ashore on some rocks below.

And so Bobolink, having been duly warned with regard to possible trouble in connection with that same hawser, had mentally called the rope his "dead line;" and he watched the shore above that point three times as much as any other place.

He and Andy had planned not to talk while on duty. If they found it necessary to say anything at all, which was hardly likely, the communication would be in the lowest whisper.

Bobolink was not greedy, but he really hoped that if any sort of trouble did come it would come along while he and Andy were holding the post of guards. He had a little fear that Spider Sexton might not be depended on, no matter what his good intentions, while Tom Betts was an unknown quantity.

In case Andy happened to be sitting in one boat, while Bobolink was occupying the other, they had fixed it up so that by taking a lead pencil, the "commander" could give a few little light taps on the side of the craft, using his knowledge of the Morse code to send the message, and in this way ask whether his assistant were wide awake, and on the job, when Andy would send back a reply along the same order; for he aspired to be a signal man of the troop, and was daily practicing with the wigwag flags, as well as smoke and fire signals.

The town clock boomed out the hour of ten.

Bobolink had himself begun to feel rather sleepy, and more to arouse his dormant faculties than anything else, he sent a message along the wooden telegraph line. The reply was a bit slow in coming, which made him think Andy might also be inclined to fall into a doze.

So Bobolink decided that he must bestir himself, and give the signal more frequently. He would not have this, his first important commission, turn out poorly, for a good deal. Perhaps his whole future usefulness as a scout who could be depended on in emergencies rested on the way he accounted for the safety of the motorboats this night.

When he found himself letting his eyes shut, even for a minute, he would immediately try to picture the consternation that would ensue should a fire suddenly envelope the boats that had been placed in the hands of the scouts, and for which they would be held responsible.

He knew Ted Slavin of old, and felt that the town bully would not hesitate at even such a thing as that.

Then there was such a thing as cutting the hawser, and letting the boats drift down-stream, to bring up against some rocks that might stave a hole in the delicate planking. Who could tell but what the rope had parted under a strain? Sometimes a break may look like the work of a sharp knife; and anyway, as darkness lay upon the scene, with a cloudy sky overhead to hide the young moon, the identity of the vandal could never be absolutely known.

All these things Bobolink was turning over and over in his mind as he sat there trying to keep awake.

It is one of the hardest things to do, and especially when the subject is only a half-grown lad, with but a dim idea of the responsibility depending on the faithful discharge of his duty.

Hello! what was that? Bobolink thought he surely heard a sound like muttered conversation. But then, even in steady old Stanhope, there were a number of happy-go-lucky chaps who tarried late in the saloons; and when they finally started homeward, used to talk to themselves along the way. Perhaps it was only one of these convivial fellows trying to find the way home, and getting off his course, coming to the open place along the river bank, intending to lie down and sleep his confusion off.

Bobolink was thrilled, however, a minute later, when he felt sure he could again hear the low mutter of voices. It struck him that several persons might be urging each other on, as though inclined to feel the need of backing.

It came from up-river, too, the point he meant to watch more than any other; and this fact increased the suspicious look of the case.

"Oh! it's coming," whispered the eager boy to himself; "and I only hope the water will be hot enough, that's all."

His words were mysterious enough to suit any one; and even while he was speaking in this manner Bobolink started to crawl under the canopy that sheltered him from the dew of the night. He allowed the end of his pencil to throb against the side of the boat, giving the one significant word: "Come!" An immediate answer assured him that Andy heard, and understood. Another minute, and the Irish boy came shuffling over from the other boat, trying to keep from making any more noise than was necessary.

"Take hold," Bobolink whispered in his ear, pulling the other's head down close to his lips; "They're coming! Be ready to go at it licketty-split when I say the word. Get that?"

"Sure!" came in the faintest tone from the other; whereupon Bobolink, feeling that his hour had arrived, started once more to crawl back to his former position.

But now he had something in his hands that looked very like a snake; or since Bobolink was known to fairly detest all crawling creatures, it might be a rope, although there are still other things that have that same willowy appearance - a garden hose, for example.

George A. Warren

CHAPTER VI

THE GREAT CRUISE OF THE SCOUTS BEGUN

When Bobolink again reached the bow of the _Comfort_, and peered above the side, he glued his eyes to the spot where he knew the rope lay that held the boats moored to the shore.

And as the half moon condescended to peep from behind the dark clouds that had until now hidden her bright face, the scout could make out a flattened figure, that seemed to be hugging the earth, while creeping slowly forward.

Not only one, but three more, did he see, all in a line, as though in this way the conspirators had arranged to keep their courage up to the sticking point. Each fellow might watch his mates, and see that no one lagged behind.

Bobolink was quivering with eagerness and excitement. He figured that these night crawlers had only five more feet to cover before they would be as close to his "dead line" as prudence would dictate that he allow, since it might require only a single sweep of the knife to cut that rope.

They kept on advancing as though anxious to get the job over with, now that they had keyed their courage up to the proper pitch.

Another foot was all that Bobolink meant to allow, and then his time would come to act. Those last few seconds seemed fairly to crawl, so wrought-up was the waiting scout; but finally he concluded that it was no use holding off any longer. So he suddenly called out the one word:

"Now!"

Instantly a new sound broke the silence. Bobolink elevated the object he was hold in his hands. There came a queer, whizzing noise, like water squirting from the end of a nozzle; which was exactly what it was, and *hot* water in the bargain, not actually scalding, but of such a temperature to make a fellow wince, if it happened to sprinkle over-his face.

It was all Bobolink's idea. He had brought a little garden pump aboard during the afternoon, with the hose that went with it. There was a kerosene cookstove aboard each boat, used when going ashore might be unwise on account of rainy weather; and on this the artful schemer had heated his water. Every time he went back to that quarter he tested its temperature, to see whether it kept up to the pitch he meant it should be. And Andy's part of the job was to manipulate the handle of the little pump with all his vim and power.

Imagine the consternation of four plotters, who, when just about to carry out their pleasant little scheme, suddenly and without warning, found a spray of hot water touching every exposed part of their skin!

Do you wonder that they immediately let out a few yelps, and scrambling to their feet, rushed headlong away, followed by the laughter and jeers of Bobolink and his hard-working assistant.

"Go it, you tigers! My! what sprinters you can be, when you only half try! Come again, when you cool off a bit! Plenty more of the same kind on tap! Don't be bashful, Teddy; let's hear from you again, and often. Whee! just listen to 'em howl, would you?"

Perhaps some of those who were with Ted Slavin in his little game were more frightened than hurt by the hot water, but they certainly did chatter as they kept on up the river bank. Little danger of them making another try to injure the boats again that night!

Of course Spider and Tom Bates had jumped up at the first outbreak, ready to help repel boarders. Their assistance was not needed; but they enjoyed the joke as much as their chums and for the next half hour all sat around, talking, and comparing notes.

But finally silence again rested over the scene; Spider and Tom condescended to crawl under their blankets again for another "cat-nap," as the former dubbed it, while Bobolink and his able assistant resumed their duties as sentries.

The night, however, was disturbed no more by any outbreak. Those would-be jokers seemed to know when they had taken hold of what Bobolink termed the "business end of a buzz-saw;" at any rate they were only conspicuous during the remainder of the night by their absence.

Of course every one of the boys on board the two motorboats was glad when the first peep of dawn came. It had seemed about "forty-eleven hours long," Spider admitted; though he also triumphantly asked Tom Betts whether the other had had occasion to jab that pin into him even once, which the second scout laughingly admitted he had not.

"See there," Spider had declared, "can't I keep awake when duty calls me? You needn't be afraid to trust a Sexton, when you need a faithful watcher."

Before the sun appeared Paul and Jack were on hand, to make sure that everything was in shape for an early start, for they hoped to get away by nine o'clock.

Others of the scouts began to drop around, and from the

appearance of their eyes Paul was of the opinion that a full night's sleep had not been enjoyed by many of the members of the troop. Of course, it was the excitement of starting out on such a glorious cruise that kept them awake; for it is not given to scouts very often to enjoy such a prospect, afloat, with staunch motorboats given over into their keeping.

Since so many things had been looked after on the preceding afternoon, there was really little to be done that morning. Every fellow was supposed to be on hand at a certain time, ready with his little blanket, and his haversack, in which he would carry a towel, some soap, a brush, an extra shirt, some socks and handkerchiefs; and if he could find a spare bit of room, why, he was entitled to cram in all the crullers or other dainties he could manage; for after that supply was gone there would be only plain camp fare until they got home again.

Paul was kept busy seeing that everything was stored away in the right place. Of course the supplies of food and the tents, as well as the numerous blankets, had to be divided as equally as possible, so that each boat would have its fair cargo.

When the roster of those who could go was taken, just before the time came to start, and the others were ordered ashore, it was found that all told there were just eighteen fellows lucky enough to be in the lot.

Some of the boys who could not go looked pretty doleful as they watched the preparations. There were the twins, William and Wallace Carberry, whose parents insisted on their going to the sea-shore; and Horace Poole, as well as Cliff Jones, of the second patrol, also compelled to obey the parental injunction; when, if given their choice, they would ten times sooner have remained at home, and had the chance of starting out on this wonderful cruise with their chums.

Sandy Griggs, the butcher's son, was laid up with a lame leg; while George Hurst happened to develop a touch of malaria, and his parents would not hear of him going on the water at such a time. As for Red Conklin and Lub Ketcham, for some reason or other which they did not care to explain, they had been positively refused permission to go along; perhaps they were being punished for some misdemeanor; and if so, to judge from the long faces they showed, the like would not be apt to happen again very soon; for it pained them dreadfully to think that they were to be debarred from all that glorious fun which the fortunate eighteen had ahead of them.

With nine to a boat there was considerable crowding; but this came mostly on account of the tremendous amount of material carried. Why, one would almost be inclined to think those boys were going off for a whole three months, instead of not more than two weeks at most, to judge from the stuff they carried. It takes boys a long time to learn to plan such trips as this in light marching order, doing without everything save absolute necessities.

Why, there was Bobolink, who ought to have known better, actually trying to get Paul to allow him to take along that little garden pump, with its line of hose. Just because it had come in so happily when those jokers meant to cut the hawser, and set the two boats adrift, Bobolink declared there could be no telling how many times it would prove a blessing; but Paul utterly refused to carry such a burden; and so in the end it was put ashore, and given in charge of the twins to return in safety to the Link garden.

When nine o'clock struck, everything seemed to be ready.

"I can't think of anything else; can you. Jack?" Paul asked his second in command, and who was to take charge of the *Speedwell*, while Paul himself ran the other craft.

"I see you've got the extra gas aboard, and that was one thing I had on my mind," replied Jack. "There's nothing else that I know. Look at William Carberry, will you? I honestly believe he's figuring in his mind right now whether he dares go, against his home order, and jump aboard, to sail with us."

"I wouldn't let him, now that I know he couldn't get permission," remarked Paul, promptly. "We want to make a start with a clean record. No fellow is going without the full permission of his folks. I'd hate to think that any scout sneaked off, and came anyhow. He wouldn't have a good time, because all the while he'd be thinking of what was coming when he got back."

"Bobolink is rubbing his chin every time he looks at that little garden pump," Jack went on, chuckling mightily, as though he enjoyed watching the faces of his comrades, and reading all sorts of things there. "He just can't see why you wouldn't let him carry it along. I heard him tell how it would be good for giving us all a clean-off shower bath, when we went in swimming; and all that sort of thing. When he can't have what he wants, Bobolink is a hard loser; isn't he, Paul?"

"Well, he beats any one else in hanging on," replied the other. "Now take those boxes that little old professor stored one night in your father's mill - Bobolink just can't get them out of his mind; and he never will be happy till you find out what was in them. After that he'll forget all about the things. But if everything is ready, I guess we might as well start."

When the *Speedwell*, being on the outside, started to "popping," and then moved off, there was a cheer from fully five score of throats; and counting the girls who had also come down to see the beginning of the motorboat cruise, there must have been nearly double that number on the bank.

Then the roomier *Comfort* also made a start, and following in the wake of the pilot boat, turned until her nose pointed down-stream. Flags were flying from fore and aft of both boats; and the boys waved their campaign hats, while they sent back hearty cheers in answer to the many good wishes shouted after them by the crowd ashore, while Bobolink blew cheery blasts on his bugle, and Bluff Shipley would have beaten a lively tattoo on his drum, only it had been decided best to leave that instrument at home.

And with all this noisy send-off, the two boats began to chug-chug down the Bushkill, bound for that far-away island in Lake Tokala, about which so many strange stories had from time to time been told.

"Well, we're off at last, Bobolink," said Jack, who had that individual aboard with him.

"That's right, and everything seems lovely, with the goose hanging high," replied the other. "But seems to me the troop owes us guards a vote of thanks for serving as we did. Just think what a lot of grunters we'd have been this fine morning, if our boats had been set adrift, and brought up on the rocks down below, with chances of holes being knocked in the sides! Say, we've got a whole lot to be thankful for, Jack; and my old garden pump stood up to the racket first-rate, too."

"That's true, Bobolink; and as soon as we're settled in camp I'm going to make sure that the troop acknowledges its indebtedness to you four fellows by a vote of thanks, see if I don't."

"Oh say, now, I didn't mean to hint that way," objected the other, turning a little red in the face with confusion. "We only did our duty, after all, if we did lose a lot of sleep. But then, I guess we got as much as a lot of the fellows that went to bed at home. Yes, we're off at last, and things look great. I'm as happy as a lark, and that free from care - well, I would be, that is, if only somebody could up and give me just a hint what those boxes had in 'em. It was so funny to have that queer professor store 'em with your father in his mill; and then to have somebody sneakin' around, wantin' to steal them. Needn't grin at me that way, Jack; you know I'm a little weak in that quarter. I sure *do* want to know! Don't suppose you've heard anything new since I talked with you last about it?" and as Jack shook his head in the negative, Bobolink looked disappointed, and turned away.

CHAPTER VII

STUCK FAST IN THE MUD

"About three mile's below Stanhope now; aren't we, Paul?" asked Jud Elderkin, the leader of the second patrol, who, with Bluff, Nuthin, Joe Clausin, Gusty Bellows, Old Dan Tucker, Phil Towns and Little Billie, constituted the crew of the *Comfort*, commanded by the scout master himself.

Jack had been given charge of the other boat, because Frank Savage was not feeling any too well, though probably he had not let his folks know about it, lest he be kept at home.

"More than that, Jud," answered the other; "and in the most ticklish part of the river, too. I ought to signal the other boat to slow up some more. You see, while there are no rocks around here, the eddies form sandbars that keep changing, just as I understand they do away out in the big Mississippi, so that a pilot on his way up-river finds a new channel cut out, and bars that were never there when he went down a week before."

"And notice, too, that Jack's given over the wheel to Bobolink, while he is back looking after the motor. Now, Bobolink is a cracker-jack of a fellow to get up all sorts of clever schemes for sprinkling creepers in the night; but he's a little apt to be flighty when it comes to running a boat. There! what did I tell you, Paul; they've run aground, as sure as you live!"

"You're right, Jud; and it looks like the *Speedwell* might go

George A. Warren

over on her beam-ends, the way she's tilted now. Good for Jack; he's ordering them all over on the upper side! That may keep her from toppling over!" Paul exclaimed, as he gave the wheel a little turn, and headed straight for the boat in peril.

"Wow! that was a right smart trick of Jack's!" cried Jud, in admiration. "If he'd lost his head, like some fellows I know might have done, nothing'd ever kept that boat on her keel. And just to think what a nasty job we'd have on our hands, trying to right her again, and before our great trip had hardly started."

"Yes," added Old Dan Tucker, who happened to be close to them, "that ain't the worst of it. You know the main part of the grub's aboard the other boat Think of those juicy hams floatin' off down the Bushkill, with not a single tooth ever bein' put in 'em; and all that bread and stuff soaked. Oh! it gives me a cold shiver to even think of it," for Dan loved the bugle call that announced dining time better than any other music.

The greatest excitement prevailed aboard both boats. Jack seemed to be keeping his crew perched along the upper rail, where their weight had the effect of holding the boat with the narrower beam from toppling over on her side. It looked like a close shave, as Jud Elderkin said, with that swift current rushing past on the port quarter, and almost lapping the rim of the cockpit.

Of course, as soon as she struck Jack had shut off power, so that the boat was now lying like a stranded little whale.

Paul brought up alongside, looking out that he did not strike the same unseen sandbar.

"Take this rope, some of you, and make fast to that cleat at the stern," Paul called out, giving a whirl that sent it aboard the tilted motorboat.

"What are you meaning to do, Paul; give us a pull back?" asked Jack, who did not seem to be one-half so "rattled" by the mishap as some of the other fellows; simply because he had the faculty of keeping his wits about him in an emergency.

"That's the only way I can see," came the reply. "And as the stern is under water, Jack, what's the matter with backing when we start to pulling?"

"Not a thing, that I can see," answered the skipper of the *Speedwell*; "But I hope she slides off all right."

"Have your crew get as far aft as they can," continued Paul. "That will lighten the bow, more or less. And keep them all on the side they're on; only as soon as she drops back on an even keel, they must get over, so she won't swing to starboard too much. All ready, now?"

"Yes, the rope's tied fast to the cleat, and unless you yank that out by the roots, the boat's just *got* to move! Say when, Paul," with which Jack again bent over the three horse-power motor with which the faster boat was equipped.

Paul took one look around before giving the word. He wanted to make sure that everything was in readiness, so there might be no hitch. A mistake at that critical stage might result in bringing about the very accident they were striving to avoid, and as a consequence it was wise to make haste slowly. That is always a rule good scout masters lay down to the boys under their charge. "Slow but sure" is a motto that many a boy would be wise to take to himself through life.

And when Paul had made certain that everything was in readiness he started the motor of the *Comfort*, reversing his lever; so that every ounce of force was exerted to drag the companion boat off its sandy bed.

Jack complied with the requirements of the situation by also starting his motor the same way; and with the happiest results.

"Hurrah! she's moving!" cried little Nuthin, who was not in danger, but just as much excited as though the reverse had been the case.

"There she comes!" yelled several of the anxious scouts, as the *Speedwell* was seen to start backward.

"One good pull deserves another; eh, fellows?" cried the delighted Bobolink, who was wondering whether Jack would ever entrust the wheel to his care again, after that accident; but he need not have worried, for somehow the skipper did not seem to feel that it was his fault.

And Bobolink, when he was again placed in charge of the wheel, felt that he had had a lesson that would last him some time. In this sort of work there could be no telling what was going to happen; hence, each scout would be wise to remember the rule by which they were supposed to always be guided, and "be prepared." That meant being watchful, wakeful, earnest, and looking for signs to indicate trouble, so that should it come they would not be caught napping.

After a little while they came in sight of Manchester, with its smoking stacks, and its busy mills. Possibly the news of the expedition of the Stanhope Troop had been carried to the boys down here. At any rate, there was a group of several fellows wearing the well known khaki-uniform, who waved to them from the bank and acted as though wishing the expedition success. They were pretty good fellows, those Manchester scouts, and the Stanhope boys liked them much more than they did the members of the Aldine troop up the river. Everybody knows there is a vast difference in boys; and sometimes even the fellows in various towns will seem, to be built along certain lines, having pretty much the same leading characteristics. The Manchester lads had proven a straightforward set in what competitions the several troops had had so far. And hence every fellow aboard the two boats swung his hat, and sent back hearty cheers.

"What's the matter with Manchester? She's all right!" they called, in unison, as Gusty Bellows took upon himself the duties which, on the ball field, made him invaluable as the "cheer captain."

His name was really Gustavus Bellows; but that was easily corrupted into Gusty when the fellows learned on his first coming to Stanhope what a tremendous voice he had.

About a mile or so below Manchester, Paul had said, the mouth of what had once been Jackson Creek, might be found. Several of the boys could remember having heard more or less about that abandoned canal; perhaps the Manchester lads knew about it, since it was closer to their home town.

Everybody, then, was anxiously scanning the shore on the left, because they knew it must lie somewhere along there.

"I see the mouth!" exclaimed Phil Towns, who had very keen eyesight. "Just look on the other side of that crooked tree, and you'll glimpse a little bar that juts out. That must be on the upper side of the creek's mouth; because Paul said bars nearly always form there. How about that, Paul?"

"Go up head, Phil; you've struck the bull's eye," replied the other, with a laugh, as he began to head in toward the crooked tree mentioned, and which doubtless he took for his landmark when in search of the creek.

The *Comfort* was in the lead now. Jack was content to play "second fiddle," as he called it. As Paul had gone through the disused canal in his canoe, exploring it pretty thoroughly, he must act as pilot.

Once they had pushed past the mouth of the creek they found a rather disheartening prospect. The water seemed very low, so that they could see bottom everywhere. Even Paul frowned, and shook his head.

"It surely must have lowered several inches since I was here yesterday," he declared, in dismay.

"Think we'll get through safely?" queried Jud Elderkin, anxiously.

"I hope we may," replied the scout master; "but we've just got to creep along, and be mighty careful. You see, most of the bed of this canal is mud, and not sand. Once the sharp bow starts to rooting in that, there's no telling how far we'll explore before letting up. And it's surprising how that same mud clings. I could hardly work my light canoe loose two or three times. Just seemed like ten pair of hands had hold of her, and were gripping tight. Easy there, Jack, take another notch in your speed, old fellow! Crawl along, if you can. And have the poles ready to fend off, if we get into any bad hole."

The boys were strung along the sides of the slowly moving motorboats. Every fellow came near holding his breath with nervousness.

"Excuse me from getting stuck here in this nasty mess," remarked Nat Smith, on board the roomier boat with Jack, Bobolink, Tom Betts, Andy Flinn, Curly Baxter, Spider Sexton, Frank Savage and Bob Tice.

"Why, we might stay here a week," observed the last mentioned, in a voice that told plainly how little he would relish such a mishap, when they had planned such splendid times ahead.

"All summer, if it didn't rain, because the creek would get lower all the time." Paul himself observed, with emphasis, wishing to make every scout resolve to avoid this catastrophe, if it were at all possible.

"Who'd ever think," remarked Jud, "that there was such a queer old place as this not more'n seven miles away from home? And not one of us ever poked a boat's nose up this same creek before Paul came down, to spy out things."

"Oh! well, there's a reason for that," replied Phil Towns, who knew all about everything that had ever happened in and around Stanhope. "Until lately, when the scouts organized in these three towns, the boys of Stanhope and those of Manchester never had much to do with each other. Many's the stone fight I've been in with those big mill chaps. Sometimes we whipped them; and then again they chased us right home. So no Stanhope boy ever dared go far down the river in the old days. That's the reason, I guess, why none of us ever tried to explore this place. Say, we seem to be getting in worse and worse, Paul. It isn't more'n a foot deep over there on the right, and less'n ten inches here on the left."

"I know it, Phil, and I'm beginning to be afraid we'll have to back out of this the best way we can," replied the scout master, reluctantly; for his heart had been set on carrying out this plan, and he hated to be compelled to give it up.

Hardly had he spoken than the boat brought up with a jolt that came near throwing several of the scouts into the water and mud. They had run aground after all! Paul turned the motor to the reverse, and the little propeller fairly sizzled in its mad efforts to drag the craft back into clear water, but it was just as Paul had said - there seemed to be innumerable hands clinging fore and aft that refused to let go. And in spite of all the work of the motor they did not move an inch.

"Rotten luck!" exploded Jud Elderkin, as he looked helplessly around, as if to see whether a fellow could at least jump ashore; but since ten feet of that ooze lay on either side, he failed to get much encouragement.

"Ahoy, *Speedwell*, you'll have to give us a lift!" called Paul, making a megaphone out of his hands.

"Y-y-yes, t-t-turn about's f-f-fair p-p-play," added Bluff, waving his bugle. "We p-p-pulled you off, and n-n-now you g-g-got to return the f-f-favor."

"Listen!" said Paul, sharply; "Jack's calling something."

And as they all lined up along the side of the *Comfort* they heard Jack's voice come across the forty feet of water and mud, saying:

"Only wish we could, Commodore; but sad to say, we're stuck about as fast in this lovely mess as you are, and can't budge her an inch!"

CHAPTER VIII

WHAT THE WATER GAUGE SHOWED

"Well, here is a pretty kettle of fish!" grunted the disgusted Jud. "We seem to take to sandbars and mud flats today to beat the band."

Paul had stopped the motor, since it seemed useless. But of course he did not mean to give up trying to get the boat off.

"One thing's sure," he said, positively, when the others gathered around him, as if in this emergency they looked to the scout master to invent some method of beating the sticky mud at its own game; "every minute we stay here makes it all the worse for us."

"Yes, because our weight is sure to make the boat sink deeper in her nest!" declared Little Billie, leaning far over the side, as if to see how far down in her muddy bed the boat lay.

"Yes, that's one thing," added Paul; "but another is the fact that the creek is falling all the time. Unless it rains, there'll soon be nothing but mud around us. Now, every fellow crowd back here, and leave the bow as free as we can. That might loosen the grip of the mud; and when I turn on the motor at full speed again, let's hope she'll move."

It was a sensible suggestion; and indeed, about the only thing possible, since the other boat, being in the same fix, could not come near, either to give a friendly tug, or take off the *Comfort's* crew.

When he had them all as far in the stern as they could get, with a warning not to allow themselves to be shaken loose, unless they wanted a mud bath, the skipper started his motor working.

When it was going at full speed the boat quivered and strained, but did not move, so far as any one could see; and they were all eager to detect the first sign of motion.

"No good!" sighed Jud. "Might as well look the thing in the face, fellows. Here we stay, and eat up all our grub, day after day. Ain't it fierce, though? How d'ye suppose we'll ever stand it? If anybody had a pair of wings now, and could fly ashore, we might get help to pull us out. But we couldn't use our wigwag flags, even if we tried, because who'd see 'em? Oh! what tough luck!"

Paul may have felt somewhat discouraged himself, but he was not the fellow to betray the fact - so early in the game, at least.

"Well, Jud," he said, soberly, "perhaps we may have to stick it out here for a while, but I hope it won't be as bad as you say. And make up your mind that if we do, it'll be a mighty strange thing, with eighteen wide awake scouts to think up all sorts of schemes and dodges that we can try."

"That's the stuff, Paul!" exclaimed Phil Towns. "Every fellow ought to get right down to hard pan, and try to think up some way of beating this old sticky mud. What's the use of being scouts, if we let a little thing like this get the better of us? If I could only wade ashore, I'd fix a hawser to a tree back there, and then by workin' the engine p'raps we might pull the boat off. I've seen 'em do that with a steamboat, away down on Indian River, when I was with my folks in Florida last winter. And it worked, too."

"Well, try the wading; it looks fine!" laughed Joe Clausin.

"Don't think of it," called out Gusty Bellows at that moment. "I stuck this pole down in the soft slush, and my stars! it goes right through to China, I reckon. Anyhow, I couldn't reach bottom. And if you jumped over, Phil, you'd be up to your neck at the start. Let's tie a rope under your arms first, anyhow."

But Paul quickly put an end to all this sort of talk.

"There's no use trying anything like that," he said. "Even if you did reach the shore, we haven't got a rope long and strong enough to do the business. Besides, we may have help soon."

With that all the boys began craning their necks, as if they expected to see some kind of a queer craft that could pass over mud as easily as other boats did water, bearing down on them, with the design of dragging them from the bank,

"Say, what does he mean? For the life of me I can't glimpse anything worth shucks; and the blooming old *Speedwell* seems to be sticking tight and fast, just the same way we are. Loosen up, Paul, and put us wise; won't you?" pleaded Phil.

"I didn't mean that any living thing was going to hold out a hand to us," remarked the smiling scout master; "but look aloft, boys, and see what's coming."

With that they followed his instructions.

A general shout went up.

"Whee! rain a-comin' down on us! Get the curtains ready to button fast, boys, or we'll have all our fine stuff soaked through and through." Little Billie called, himself setting things in motion by seizing one of the rolled curtains, and letting it come down, to be fastened around the cockpit by means of gummets and screws.

"But Paul meant something else," declared Jud Elderkin, wisely. "You see, if only that rain does come, and it's heavy enough, there's going to be a lot more water in this old canal than we need to pull through with. You know how quick the Bushkill River rises; and I guess it's the same way with the Radway."

"Oh! don't we wish that there'll just be a little old cloud-burst!" cried Gusty Bellows. "I could stand anything but staying here seven or ten days, doin' nothing, only eat, and stare at this mud, and wish I was back home. Come on, little clouds; get a move on you, and let's hear you growl like thunder."

They had by now called the attention of the others to the prospects for rain. Indeed, as soon as the first curtain fell, some of Jack's crew took note of the significant fact, and they could be seen looking up at the blackening heavens. There had been very few times in the past when those boys had hoped it would rain. Perhaps, when they were kept home from a picnic - for reasons - some of them may have secretly wished the clouds would let down a little flood, so that those who had been lucky enough to go, might not have such a laugh on them after all.

But certainly they never felt just as they did now, while watching the play of those gathering storm clouds.

"And the best of the joke is," commented Jud, with a grin, "that lots of the good folks at home right now are looking up at those same black clouds, and pitying us boys. They don't realize how we're just praying that the rain won't turn out a fizzle, after all. Wasn't that a drop I felt?"

[Transcriber's note: Beginning of sentence missing from original text] till that gray gets nearly overhead," remarked Paul, pointing up at a line marked across the heavens about half-way toward the horizon, and in the direction of the wind.

"It's getting dark, anyway," remarked Nuthin, rather timidly;

for truth to tell, the small boy had never ceased to remember how, earlier in the season, when in camp up near Rattlesnake Mountain, a terrible storm had struck them and as he clung desperately to the tent they were trying to hold down, he had actually been carried up into the branches of a tree, from which position only the prompt work of his fellow scouts had finally rescued him.

"And look at that flash of lightning, would you?" echoed Joe Clausin. "Wow! that was a heavy bang; wasn't it? Tell you now, that bolt must 'a struck somethin'! Always does, they say, when it comes quick like that."

"How's the cover; just as snug as you can make it, boys?" demanded Paul; "because we'll likely get a bit of a blow first, before the rain comes, and it'd be a bad job if we lost this whole business. Stand by to grab hold wherever you can. After that, if we weather it all right, there'll be no trouble."

"And say, she's coming licketty-split, believe me," called Jud. "I c'n hear it hummin' through the trees over there like the mischief. Take hold, everybody; and don't let it get away from you!"

"We'll all go up together this time, then!" muttered little Nuthin; but with the grit that seemed a part of his nature, once he started in to do anything, he also seized the canvas covering at the bottom, and set his teeth hard.

With a roar the wind struck them. Had it come from the right quarter Paul believed it might have helped work them loose; but it happened unfortunately that just the reverse was the case. If anything, they were driven on the mud-bank all the harder.

But at any rate the tarpaulin canopy did not break loose, and that was something to be satisfied with.

The wind whooped and howled for perhaps three minutes.

Then it died down, as if giving up the attempt to tear the boat's top out of the hands of the determined boys.

"The worst's over, fellows!" called Paul, breathing hard.

"Hurrah! that's better'n saying it is yet to come. How'd the *Speedwell* make out?" Jud asked, sinking back on a thwart, the better to find some place to peep out.

"Seems to be all there," replied Nuthin, who had been quicker to look than the more clumsy Jud. "She's got her cover on, and I guess that means they're safe and sound; but she don't seem to be floatin' worth a cent.

"No more are we; but listen, there comes the rain. Now for it," observed Paul, as with a rush the water began to descend, rattling on the roof of the canopy cover.

"Fine! Keep right along that way for a while, and something's bound to get a move on it, which I hope will be our two boats!" cried Gusty Bellows.

"Did you ever hear it come down heavier than that?" demanded Old Dan Tucker, as he looked anxiously around to see that none of the cargo was exposed to the flood.

"Wonder if this old thing sheds water?" suggested Jud, looking up at the heavy canopy as though he fancied that he felt a stream trickling down the back of his neck.

"You can bank on it," declared Joe Clausin. "Anything Mr. Everett owns has got to be gilt-edged. And he'd never stand for a leaky canopy. What're you lookin' at out there, Paul?" for the scout master was leaning a little out on the side away from their companion boat in misery.

"Why, you see," replied the scout master, drawing his head back, "I fixed a little contrivance here, just before the storm broke, and I'm looking now to see whether it shows the least gain in water. I marked this pole with inches, and rammed it just so far in the mud. If the water starts to rising any, I can tell as soon as I look."

"And is she going up yet?" asked Jud, eagerly,

"Well, it wouldn't be fair to expect that for some time yet," replied Paul. "At the best I expect we'll have to stay here an hour or so, until the water up-stream has a chance to come down. I hope it may surprise me, and get here quicker than that. And boys, if we have to spend all that time doing nothing, why we might try that little oil stove Mr. Everett has, and see how it can get us a pot of coffee, with our cold lunch."

"What time is it now?" asked Jud; while Old Dan Tucker pricked up his ears, at the prospect of "something doing" along his favorite line.

"Going on eleven; and I had my breakfast awful early!" remarked Little Billie.

"And I had hardly a bite - reckon I was too much excited to eat - so I'm mighty near starved right now," declared Dan Tucker; but then the boys had known him to put up that same sort of a plea only an hour after devouring the biggest meal possible, so they did not expect to see him collapse yet awhile from weakness through lack of food.

All the same, Paul agreed that it might serve to distract their minds if they did have lunch. He also asked Jud to get in communication with those on the other boat, if the rain had let up enough for them to exchange signals, and by means of the flag, tell them what those on the *Comfort* meant to do.

Just as Bobolink, who answered, had informed them that those under Jack were about to follow the same course, Paul took another glance at his rude water gauge.

When he drew in his head, Jud, who had been waiting to tell

what the others reported, saw that Paul was smiling as though pleased.

"What's doing, Commodore?" he asked.

"The water has risen half an inch, and is still going up," replied Paul.

At that there was a roar of delight - only Old Dan Tucker was so busy watching the lunch being got ready, he did not seem to hear the joyous news.

CHAPTER IX

ON THE SWIFT RADWAY

"Let me work my flags a little, and tell the other boat the news!" suggested Jud; and as no one objected he got busy.

It was good practice, and he had something worth while to communicate, so Jud enjoyed the task.

By the time he was through, lunch was ready, the coffee having boiled enough to please the most critical among the boys.

"Rain seems to be letting up some," remarked Gusty Bellows, as they gathered around to discuss what was to be their first meal of the trip.

"Oh! I hope it isn't going to tantalize us, and raise our hopes only to dash 'em down again," said Gusty.

"From the signs I don't think we're through with it all yet," Paul observed; and as they had considerable faith in the acting scout master as a weather prophet, there arose a sigh of satisfaction at this remark.

"Take a look, and see if she's still moving up the scale, Paul," begged the anxious Phil Towns.

When this had been done, there was a look of eager expectancy on every face.

George A. Warren

"Over a full inch since the start," Paul reported.

"And that's nearly half an hour back," complained Gusty. "Gee! if it goes up as slow as that, we'll be camping here at sun-down, sure, fellers."

"Oh! I don't know," Paul put in, confidently; "you must remember that the rain has fallen all over the watershed that supplies both these rivers; and this canal now serves as a link between the two. If either one rises a good deal, we're just bound to get the benefit of that little flood. Even at an inch an hour we could be moving out of this before a great while. And I expect that the rise will do better than that, presently. Just eat away, and wait. Nothing like keeping cool when you just have to."

"Yes, when you tumble overboard, like I did once on a time," chuckled Jud. "I kept perfectly cool; in fact, none of you ever saw a cooler feller; because it was an ice-boat I dropped out of; and took a header into an open place on the good old Bushkill. Oh! I can be as cool as a cucumber - when I have to."

An hour later Paul announced that the rise had not only kept up as he predicted, but was increasing.

"Here's good news for you, fellows," he remarked, after examining his post, "if it keeps on rising like it's doing right now, we'll be starting in less than another hour!"

"Whoopee! that suits me!" cried Gusty, enthusiastically.

"Ditto here," echoed Jud. "I never was born for inaction; like to be doing something all the time."

"So do I," Paul observed, quietly; "but when I find myself blocked in one direction I just turn in another, and take up some other work. In that way I manage not only to keep busy, but to shunt off trouble as well. Try it some time, Jud, and I give you my word you'll feel better."

But that next hour seemed very long to many of the impatient boys. They even accused the owner of the watch of having failed to wind it on the preceding night, just because it did not seem inclined to keep pace with their imagination.

The water was rising steadily, if slowly, and some of them declared that there was now a perceptible motion to the boat whenever they moved about.

Urged on by an almost unanimous call, Paul finally agreed to start the motor again, and see what the result would be. So Jud sent the order to the second boat by means of his signal flags.

When the cheerful popping of the _Comfort's_ exhaust made itself heard, there was an almost simultaneous cheer from the scouts.

"We're off!" they shouted, in great glee.

"Goodbye, old mud bank!" cried Gusty, waving his hand in mock adieu to the unlucky spot where so much precious time had been wasted. "See you later!"

"Not much we will!" echoed Joe Clausin. "I've got that spot marked with a red cross in my mind, and if this boat ever gets close to it again, you'll hear this chicken cackle right smart. It's been photographed on my brain so that I'll see it lots of times when I wake up in the night."

"How about the other boat?" asked Paul, who was stooping down to fix something connected with the motor at the time, and could not stop to look for himself, although he could hear the throbbing of the *Speedwell's* machinery.

"Oh! she slid off easier than we did, I reckon," remarked Old Dan Tucker, now snuggled down comfortably, and apparently in a mood to take things easy, since it would be a long time between "eats."

"Tell them to go slow, all the same, Jud," Paul remarked.

"You don't seem to trust this creek as much as you might, Paul?" chuckled Gusty, who was handling the wheel, during the minute that Paul was busy.

"Well, after that experience I confess that I'm a little suspicious of all kinds of mud banks. They're the easiest things to strike up an acquaintance with, and a little the hardest to say goodbye to, of anything I ever met. Give her a little twist to the left, Gusty. That place dead ahead don't strike me as the channel. That's the ticket. I guess we missed another slam into a waiting mud bank. Now I'll take the wheel again, if you don't mind."

"Rain's over!" announced Little Billie.

"Looks like it, with that break up yonder," Jud remarked, glancing aloft. "Hope so, anyhow. We've had all the water we needed, and if it kept on coming we'd be apt to find things kind of damp up there at the island."

The mention of that word caused several of the boys to glance quickly at each other. It was as though a shiver had chased up and down their spinal columns. For Joe and Little Billie, and perhaps Gusty Bellows, were not quite as easy in their minds about that "ghost-ridden" island as they might have been; although, if taken to task, all would doubtless have stoutly denied any belief in things supernatural.

The *Comfort* acted as the pilot boat, and led the way, slowly but surely, with the *Speedwell* not far behind. The latter had one or two little adventures with flirting mud banks, but nothing serious, although on each occasion the cries of dismay from the crew could be plainly heard aboard the leading craft.

And so they came in sight of a river that had a decided current, after the smart shower had added considerably to its flow. By now the sun was shining, and the rain clouds had about vanished, being "hull-down" in the distance, as Jud expressed it; for since they were now on a voyage, he said that they might as well make use of such nautical terms as they could remember.

"That's the roaring Radway, I take it," observed Gusty, as all of them caught glimpses of the river through the trees ahead.

"Just what it is," replied Paul; "and as it has quite a strong current, we're going to have our hands full, pushing up the miles that lie between here and our camping place."

"But we c'n do it before dark; can't we, Paul?" asked Phil Towns.

"Sure we can, if nothing happens to knock us out," said Gusty, before the other could reply. "Why, we've got several hours yet, if we did have such tough luck in the blooming old canal."

"We ought to be mighty glad we got off as as easy as we did, that's what!" declared Old Dan Tucker, who was something of a philosopher in his way, and could look at the bright side as well as the next one, always providing the food supply held out.

Ten minutes later the *Comfort* was in Radway River, headed up-stream. Just as Paul had said, the current proved very swift, and while the little motor worked faithfully and well, their progress was not very rapid.

Besides, it kept them always on the watch. No one was acquainted with the channel, and the presence of rocks might not always be detected from surface indications. Some of the treacherous snags were apt to lie out of sight, but ready to give them a hard knock, and perhaps smash a hole in the bow.

And so Paul stationed two boys in positions where they could watch for every suspicious eddy, which was to be brought to his attention immediately it was discovered.

An hour passed, and they were still moving steadily up the river. Paul, in reply to many questions by his impatient comrades, announced that to the best of his knowledge they ought to arrive at their destination an hour and more before dark; which pacified the croakers, who had been saying the chances were they would have to spend their first night on the bank, short of the island by a mile or more.

"That's all right," Old Dan Tucker had remarked; "just so long as we get ashore in time to build our cooking fire, it suits me."

Everything seemed to be moving along with clock-like regularity, the boat breasting the current and throwing the spray in fine style, when Jud gave a cry.

"Something's happened to the *Speedwell*!" he announced.

Of course every eye was instantly turned back, and they were just in time to see something that announced the truth of Jud's assertion.

Andy Flinn stood up in the bow of the second boat, which no longer chugged away as before, and he threw something out that splashed in the water.

"It's their anchor!" cried Jud. "Either somebody's overboard, or else their motor's broken down!"

"It's the motor, I guess," Paul observed. "Get out our anchor, and follow suit."

CHAPTER X

DODGING THE SNAGS AND THE SNARES

A minute later both motorboats lay anchored in the middle of the swift-flowing Radway, and about sixty feet apart.

"What's the matter?" shouted Jud, taking it upon himself to learn the facts in the quickest possible time, so that signal flags were not used.

"Something's happened to our motor; but Jack thinks he can fix her up, given a little time," came in the voice of Bobolink.

"Well, call on us if we can help out any," Paul shouted; for the slapping of the water against the sides of the boat, as well as over the stones on either hand, made it hard to hear plainly.

"What if they can't fix the motor up?" remarked Phil Towns; "I hope that won't mean we've got to spend the whole night out here in the middle of the river."

"Oh I if it comes to the worst, we can tow her ashore; and then it's camp on the river bank for ours," announced Paul, cheerfully. He always seemed to have plans made up in advance, as though anticipating every trouble that could arise, and getting ready for it.

"Huh! that mightn't be so bad, after all," grunted Joe Clausin; and even Gusty Bellows and Little Billie nodded their heads, as if agreeing that there were things less desirable than camping on the bank.

The minutes dragged along, until half an hour had gone. Even Paul began to show signs of restlessness. He finally made a megaphone of his hands, and called to Bobolink:

"Tell Jack to step up; I'd like to ask him a question or two."

"Ay, ay, sir," replied the other, touching his forelock in true man-o'-war style, and immediately the head of Jack appeared.

"What's the good word, Jack?" asked the Commodore of the expedition. "Can you make the mend, d'ye think; and just about how long is it going to take you?"

"Between five and ten minutes, not more," came the reply; "I've got the hang of it now, and the end's in sight."

"Whoopee! that sounds good to me!" shouted Gusty Bellows, waving his hat.

Five minutes had hardly passed before they heard the familiar pop-pop-pop of the *Speedwell's* motor exhaust.

"How is it?" called Paul once more.

"Fine and dandy," answered Bobolink, waving his bugle; and giving a few vigorous blasts to indicate that victory was nigh.

"They're hauling in the anchor, which is a good sign," declared Nuthin.

Presently both boats were again breasting the stream. Apparently no serious result had come from the accident, save that more than a good half-hour had been wasted. But still Paul declared that he had hopes of making their destination before darkness set in.

The sun was getting very low, and the river looked desolate indeed. It was bordered by swampy land; and where the ground showed, there seemed to be such a vast number of rocks that farming had never been attempted.

"What d'y'e suppose is in those marshes?" Gusty asked, after they had passed about the fifth.

"I understand that a lot of cranberries are gathered here every Fall, and sent down to the cities for the market," Jud Elderkin replied.

"And seems to me a bear was killed last year somewhere up here," Nuthin' put in, rather timidly. "So I'm glad you brought that gun along, Paul. We are not lookin' for a bear, because we never lost one; but if he *did* come to camp it'd be nice to feel that we could give the old chap a warm reception."

"Huh! I can see the warm reception he'd get," chuckled Jud. "Seventeen trees would each one have a scout sitting up in the branches as quick as hot cakes. Guess Paul would have to be the reception committee all alone."

"Don't you believe it," remarked Gusty Bellows; "You'd see me making for the axe in a *big* hurry, I believe in an axe. It makes one of the greatest weapons for defence you ever saw. I've practiced swinging it around, and I know just how to strike."

"Well, we'll remember that; won't we, fellows?" remarked Jud, with a laugh. "Plenty of axe exercise Gusty needs, to keep him in trim for bears; and I can see now how our firewood is going to be attended to."

They kept pushing on all the while; and there was never a time that the lookout did not have to keep his eyes on the alert, because of the traps and snares that lay in wait for the voyagers up the rough Radway.

"Great river, I don't think!" Joe Clausin ventured to remark, after they had done considerable dodging, to avoid a mass of rocks that blocked the way in a direct line.

"Still, you'll notice that there's always a passage around," said Paul. "It's that way with nearly everything. Lots of times we don't see the opening till we get right on it, and then all of a sudden, there's the path out."

"I guess you're right, Paul," observed Joe. "Things do happen to a fellow sometimes, in a funny way, and just when he feels like giving up, he sees the light. You remember a lot of trouble I had once, and how it turned out splendidly? And so I learned my lesson, I sure did. I look at things different now. It showed me how silly it is to worry over things that you can't help."

"But all the same," remarked Gusty, "I wish we had a squint at that same old lake ahead. It's getting sunset, and beyond, Paul."

"I know it, and we must be pretty near the place now," replied the scout master. "Unless we see it inside of ten minutes I'll have to give the word to turn in to the shore at the next half-way decent landing, where there seems to be enough water to float our boats."

"There's a good place right now," declared Joe, pointing; "and we mightn't run across as fine a landing again."

"Ten minutes, I said," repeated Paul, positively; because he believed that there were certain signs to tell him they would come in sight of the big lake, from which the Radway flowed, after they had turned the next bend.

Somehow the others seemed to guess what he had in mind, and all were anxiously watching as they drew near the bend.

As the trees ceased to shut out their view, they gave a shout of delight, for the lake was there, just as Paul had anticipated.

"Whew! she's a big place, all right!" declared Jud, as they looked toward the distant shore, where the trees seemed lost in the shadows.

"I never dreamed there was a lake like this so near Stanhope," declared Joe, as he stared. "That one up by Rattlesnake Mountain could be put in a corner of Tokala, and wouldn't be missed. And say, that must be the island over yonder; don't you think so, Paul?"

"Look and see if you can sight a cedar growing on the top of the hill that they say stands in the middle of the island," suggested the scout master, still busy at the wheel; for the danger was not yet all over, as they had not entered the lake itself, though very near.

"It's there, all to the good!" announced Jud.

"Anybody could see that" added Gusty, who was a little jealous of the superior eyesight of several of his comrades, he being a trifle near-sighted.

"Well, if we are going to make a job of it, the sooner it's over the better," was the queer remark Joe made; but no one paid any particular attention to his words, they were so taken up with watching the island.

And so the leading motorboat left the noisy waters of the Radway, and glided into the smoother lake, much to the satisfaction of the crew; for the boys had grown tired of the constant need of watchfulness in avoiding reefs and snags.

Paul shut off power, and waited to see whether the companion boat succeeded in reaching the calm waters of the big lake as successfully as they had done. As it was now pretty close to dark, in spite of the half-moon that hung overhead, seeing the partly hidden rocks was not an easy task.

And so he watched with not a little concern the progress of the

George A. Warren

Speedwell during those last few minutes. But Jack was alive to the situation; and managed to bring his boat safely through, being greeted with a cheer from those on board the waiting *Comfort.*

"Now it's straight for the island!" called out Bobolink, as the boats drew together, and the motors started as cheerfully as if they had not undergone a hard day's work from the time the voyagers left Stanhope.

"We'll have to make camp by firelight, that's plain," grumbled Gusty.

"What's the odds, so long as we get fairly comfortable for the night?" Bobolink retorted, being one of the kind who can make the best of a bad bargain when necessary. "All we want to do is to get the tents up and a fire going, so we can cook something. Then in the morning we'll do all the fancy fixing you can shake a stick at, and try out all the new wrinkles every fellow's had in mind since our last camp. This is what I like. A lake for me, with an island in it that nobody lives on, but p'raps an old wildcat or a she bear with cubs."

"But they say something *does* live on it, and that he's a terror too; a real wild man that's got hair all over him like a big baboon - I heard it from a man that saw him once, and he wouldn't lie about it either," Joe Clausin called out.

Although the rest of the scouts mocked him, and pretended to jeer at the idea of such a thing as a wild man existing so near Stanhope, nevertheless, as the two motorboats gradually shortened the distance separating them from the mysterious island, they gazed long at the dark mass lying on the still water of the big lake and its gloomy appearance affected them.

Just as Joe Clausin had said, it had a real "spooky" air, that, at the time, with night at hand, did not impress them very favorably.

CHAPTER XI

THE CAMP ON CEDAR ISLAND

It was with extreme caution that the two motor-boats crept along the shore of the island, with numerous eyes on the lookout for a good landing place.

"Seems to be plenty of water right here," remarked Jud, who was sounding with one of the poles. "Eight feet, if an inch, Paul."

Paul shut off the power immediately.

"And this looks like the best sort of place to make our landing," he said. "If we don't like it, or find a better for a permanent camp in the morning, we can change. Get busy with the poles, fellows, and shove the boat alongside that bank there."

This was readily done, and Jud was the first to jump ashore. He wanted to be able to say that of the whole troop he had landed before any one else, ghost or no ghost.

Soon the others followed suit, even if Joe and Little Billie - and yes, Gusty Bellows also looked timidly around. There was Nuthin, always reckoned a rather timorous chap, showing himself indifferent to spirits, and all such things. What bothered Nuthin concerned material things, like cats, and dogs, and wandering bears; he snapped his fingers at spooks, because he had never seen one, and did not believe in "fairy stories," as he called them, anyway.

As the second boat came alongside, and her crew swarmed over the side, there were plenty of hands to do things, though they naturally looked to Paul for orders.

"A fire, first, fellows!" called out the scout master; "so we can see what we're doing. Because it's getting pretty dark around here, with these trees overhead. Jud, you take charge of that part, and the rest gather wood."

Many hands make light work, and in what Bobolink called a "jiffy" there came plenty of wood of all kinds, from dead branches to small-sized logs.

Jud, like every true scout, knew just how to go about starting a fire. True, the recent rain had wet pretty much all of the wood, so that a tenderfoot would have had a difficult task getting the blaze started, though after that trouble had been surmounted it would not be so bad. But Jud knew just how to split open a log, and find the dry heart that would take fire easily; and in a brief time he had his blaze springing up.

Then others began to bring some of the things ashore, particularly the tents, in which they expected to sleep during their stay.

Most of the boys were deeply impressed by the size of both the lake and the island; since they had not dreamed that things would be upon such a large scale.

Then there was that strange silence, broken only by the constant murmur of the water passing out, where the Radway River had its source; and perhaps, when a dry spell lowered the water of the lake, even this might not be heard.

It seemed to some of the scouts as though they were isolated from all the rest of the world, marooned in a desolate region, and with many miles between themselves and other human beings.

However, when the white tents began to go up, as the several squads of workers took hold in earnest, things began to look more cheerful. There is nothing that chases away the "blues" quicker than a cheerful fire, and the sight of "homey" tents.

"In the morning, if we feel like it, we can put up a flagstaff in front, and fly not only our banner, but Old Glory as well," Paul observed. "And now, suppose some of you fellows give me a hand here."

"What you going to do, Paul?" asked Old Dan Tucker, eagerly.

"Begin to get supper," came the answer.

"I'll give you a hand there," said the other.

"Me too," said Nat Smith, who was a clever cook.

And when the odor of coffee began to steal through the camp, the boys felt amply repaid for all they had undergone in the rough trip from Stanhope. They sniffed the air, and smiled, and seemed ready to declare the expedition a great success.

More than that, the cooks being blessed with healthy appetites themselves, had cut generous slices from one of the fine hams, and these were also on the fire, sizzling away at a great rate, and throwing off the most tempting odors imaginable.

It was a happy sight about that time, and showed the best side of camp life. All of the boys belonging to the Red Fox Patrol at least, had been through the mill before, and knew that there was another side to the picture; when the rain descended, and the wind blew with hurricane force, possibly tearing the canvas out of their hands, and leaving them exposed to the storm, to be soaked through.

But of course they hoped nothing of that sort was going to happen to them on this trip. Once a year ought to be enough.

If the season of preparation was delightful, what shall be said of that time when the eighteen boys sat around in favorite attitudes, each with a cup of steaming coffee beside him, to which he could add sugar and condensed milk to suit his taste; while on his knees he held a generous-sized tin pannikin, upon which was heaped a mess of friend potatoes and ham, besides all the bread he could dispose of?

"This is the stuff; it's what I call living!" Bobolink remarked.

"You never said truer words." mumbled Old Dan Tucker, who was about as busy as a beaver, his eyes sparkling with satisfaction.

"One thing sure!" declared Spider; "when Dan stops eating, he'll quit living."

"Huh! guess all of us will," added Curly Baxter.

They were in no hurry to finish the feast; and when the end did arrive, it would take a microscope to discover any crumbs left over.

"The worst is yet to come," announced Jud, "and that's washing up."

But all these things had been arranged for beforehand, so that in due course of time every fellow would have his share of camp duties. Today he might have to assist in the cooking; tomorrow help wash dishes; the next day be one of the wood-getters; and then perhaps on the fourth blissful day, he would be at liberty to just loaf!

And no doubt that last day was the one most of them would be apt to enjoy above all else; for otherwise they would hardly have been flesh and blood boys.

While those whose duty lay in cleaning up after the meal were engaged, some of the others joined Paul in bringing the blankets ashore, and distributing them to the various tents.

There were three of the latter, which would allow of six boys to each, perhaps a rather "full house" - but then they could curl up and not take much room.

"Aren't we going to keep any watch, Paul?" asked Joe Clausin, when later on some of the more tired talked of turning in.

"Watch for what?" demanded Bobolink.

"Guess Joe thinks Ted Slavin and his crowd might get over here, and throw stones at our tents, like they did once before," suggested Nuthin.

"Well, they do say there's a wild man around here," declared Joe, in a half hesitating way; for he was actually ashamed to expose his belief in supernatural things for fear of being laughed at.

"Let Mr. Wild Man come around; who cares?" sang out Bobolink. "Why, the circuses are always wantin' wild men, you know; and I guess we'd get a pretty hefty sum now, if we could capture this wonderful critter that's been living here so long covered with the skins of wild beasts he's ate up. It's me to hit the rubber pillow I fetched along. And Joe, if you want to watch, nobody is going to keep you from doing it"

And with these words Bobolink dodged into the tent that he knew his mess belonged to; in which action he was followed by numerous other scouts. Joe, finding himself left in the lurch, cast a fearful glance around at the heavy growth of timber on one side the camp, the lake being on the other; after which he shook his head as though the prospect of sitting there by the dying fire did not appeal very much to him - and crawled under the flap, too.

Perhaps it could hardly be said that silence rested on the scene; for with a dozen and a half boys trying to get to sleep there is always more or less horseplay. But an hour later, something like quiet settled down. The fire was dying out, too, since they had no reason for keeping it going, the night air being balmy.

Midnight came and went, and it must have been toward two o'clock in the morning when every boy suddenly sat upright, as though a galvanic shock had passed in and out of every tent.

So it had, for the very earth trembled under them, as a terrific detonation sounded, just as though a bolt of lightning had struck a nearby tree. And some of the scouts were ready to declare that the shock had been accompanied by a brilliant electric flash, that almost blinded them.

Immediately there began to be an upheaval, as blankets were tossed aside and the scouts crawled or scrambled from under, uttering all sorts of exclamations, and apparently too dazed to account for the phenomenon.

They began to swarm out of the tents, and loud were the outcries of astonishment when they discovered not a cloud as big as a hand in the starry heavens.

CHAPTER XII

WAS IT A BURSTING METEOR?

"Who hit me?" exclaimed Bobolink, rubbing his eyes as he gained his feet and looked around at the dimly-seen forms of the other scouts; for the moon had by now sunk behind the horizon.

"What busted?" demanded Nuthin. "I bet it was that bottle of raspberry vinegar my sister put in my knapsack. It's gone sour, and exploded, sure as anything."

Strange to say, none of the others even bothered laughing at such a foolish remark as this. They stared at the clear sky overhead, and the twinkling stars looking down upon them, just as though winking to each other, and enjoying the confusion of the valiant scouts.

Even Paul, who generally knew everything, seemed mystified.

"I declare if I can tell what it was," he said upon being appealed to by some of the others in the group. "I was sound asleep, like the rest of you, when all of a sudden it seemed as if the end of the world had come. I felt the ground shake under me and as I opened my eyes it seemed as if I was nearly blinded. The flash came and went just like lightning, and that bang was what would pass for thunder in a storm; but for the life of me I can't see any sign of trouble up there."

George A. Warren

"And we don't hear anything more; do we?" demanded Jud.

"Sounded like a big cannon to me," remarked Jack.

"Couldn't be that the State troops are out, and having manoeuvres, with a sham battle, could it?" questioned Gusty Bellows.

"Well, hardly, without somebody knowing about it. And they generally take up that sort of thing later in the year. There's only one explanation that sounds a bit reasonable to me," Paul went on.

"Tell us what that is, then?" asked Bobolink.

"I've heard about meteors falling, and exploding when they hit the earth," the scout master went on to say.

"That's right!" echoed Jack; "and say, they're always accompanied by a dazzling light, as they shoot through space, burning the air along with them. Yes, siree, that must have been a big meteor stone."

"Then it struck the earth right close to our camp, mark me," vowed Jud.

"Ain't I glad it didn't pick out this spot to drop on," crowed Nuthin. "Whew! guess we'd have been squashed flatter than that pancake you hear about."

"What are meteors made up of - they drop from stars; don't they?" asked Bob Tice.

"Oh! there's just millions and billions of 'em flying around loose," said Phil Towns, who liked to read of astronomy at times. "Lots of 'em happen to get caught in the envelope of air that surrounds the earth. Then they fall victims to the force of gravitation, and come plunging down at such speed that they do really burn the air, just like Jack said. You see, they're made up for the most part of metals, and our old earth draws 'em like a monster magnet."

"Is that what shooting stars are?" Bob went on to ask.

"Why, yes, they're really small meteors. We often pass through a mess of 'em. I've counted hundreds in a single night," Phil continued, always willing to give any information he could along his favorite study.

"Well, they say lightning don't strike in the same place twice; and that goes with your old buzzing meteors too, I reckon; so what's the use in our staying up any longer?" remarked Bobolink, who seemed quite satisfied with the explanation Paul had given of the queer noise, and the flash of brilliant light.

So they crawled back into their snug nests, and tried to compose themselves for sleep. But it is extremely doubtful whether a single one of those eighteen boys secured so much as a decent cat-nap between that hour and dawn.

Despite their apparent belief in the explanation of the phenomenon advanced by Paul, the boys could not get rid of the notion that that tremendous crash had something to do with the strange things told about the haunted island, and which helped to give it its bad name.

They were up pretty early, too. The first birds were beginning to chirp in the brush when figures came crawling out of the tents, with a great stretching of arms, and long yawns.

Then the lake tempted many of the boys, and a great splashing announced that those who could swim were enjoying a morning dip while others were taking a lesson in learning the first rudiments in the art; for Paul wanted every scout in Stanhope Troop to be able to swim and dive before the Fall came on.

The scout master himself watched the proceedings, hardly able to get his own dip because of his anxiety concerning those who, for the time being, had been placed in his charge.

This thing of being responsible for seventeen lively boys is not all that it may be cracked up to be; especially if the acting scout master is a conscientious chap, alive to his duties. Paul felt the weight of the load; but he did not shrink.

Breakfast was presently under way, and nobody found any fault when Bobolink announced that he meant to instruct Nat Smith and another boy just how to go about making those delicious flapjacks for which he himself had become famous.

In the cooking contests, at the time the Stanhope Troop carried off their banner in competition with the troops of Manchester and Aldine, Bobolink had easily outclassed all rivals when it came to the science of camp cookery, and his flapjacks were admitted without a peer, so that ever since, when the boys had an outing, there was always a shout when it was found that Bobolink was willing to get a mess of cakes ready for their attention.

Although most of the boys had looked a bit peaked, and even haggard, when they first issued from the tents, this had long since vanished. The frolic in the cool water, and now this feast in the open, proved the finest tonics possible.

They were now filled with new energy and pluck. Nobody dreamed of being frightened away from camp by such a little thing as a meteor bursting near by, or any other strange happening. Perhaps, when night came around again, this buoyant feeling might take wings, and fly away; but then, there would be fourteen and more hours before darkness again assailed them, and what was the use fretting over things so far removed?

All had made up their minds to do a lot of things while up at camp, according to their various tastes. One began to look around for subjects he could take snapshots of, having a liking for photography. Another got a companion to take up a station along the shore, so that they could exchange messages, using the flags and the code.

Then there were several who evinced a decided interest in finding the tracks of wild animals, like a raccoon, or a rabbit, or even a squirrel, when nothing better presented itself. These they minutely examined, and applied all sorts of theories in forming the story of the trail. In many cases these proved very entertaining indeed, and Paul was always pleased, with Jack's assistance, to pass on such things, being adapted through practical experience to correct errors, and set the beginner straight on certain facts that he had mixed.

There were numerous other things to do also. One boy loved to hunt wild flowers, and as soon as he could coax a mate to accompany him, since Paul would not allow the scouts to go off alone, he busied himself in the undergrowth, looking in mossy spots for some of the shy blossoms that appealed to his collecting taste.

Another seemed to have a love for geology. He wanted to find specimens of every sort of stone, and hinted of certain stories of mining having been carried on in these regions a century or two ago. But as he did not find any ore that contained precious minerals in paying quantities, during their stay on Cedar Island, the chances are that his father will still have to go right along paying his bills, even after he gets into college later in life.

The morning was slipping away fast, and they had not found any better place to settle on for a camp. It seemed that, by the merest chance, they had hit upon the best spot for a short stay on the island.

Three of the boys wandered along the shore, fishing. Paul had seen them pull in several good-sized bass, and began to make up his mind that after all they were going to have a fish dinner, if the luck held. He was even debating whether he dared leave camp for a while, and taking his jointed rod, joined the trio who had wandered around the bend of the eastern shore of the island; for Paul certainly did love to feel a lively fish at the end of his line, and could not think of leaving Lake Tokala without giving its finny inhabitants a chance to get acquainted with him.

Just as he had about decided that he could be spared for the hour that still remained until noon, Paul thought he heard a shout. Now, the scouts had more than a few times given tongue during the morning, when engaged in some boisterous game; but it struck Paul, whose nerves were always on the alert for such things, while this responsibility rested on his shoulders, that there was certainly a note, as of alarm, about this particular outcry.

It seemed to come from around that bend, too, where he had seen the three boys disappear. Even as he looked in that direction, he saw something come in sight among the rocks that lay so thickly around. It was Gusty Bellows, one of the anglers; yes, and there was Little Billie just behind him, taking great leaps that promised to speedily leave the other far in the lurch.

Paul's heart seemed to stand still. Where was Jud, who had been in the company of the two? What could have happened?

The scout master dropped his rod, which he had been in the act of jointing, and started on a run to meet the two fishermen; for he could hear them shouting, though unable to distinguish just what they were saying.

CHAPTER XIII

THE FOOTPRINTS IN THE SAND

Then Paul felt a sensation of sudden relief pass over him. He had discovered a third figure running, some distance in the rear of the other scouts; and when he recognized this as Jud Elderkin, he knew that whatever might have happened to frighten the fishermen, at least none of them seemed to be in any immediate danger.

Of course, by this time scouts were springing up all around, and all heading toward the common centre, which would be where Paul and the fishermen must meet.

Little Billie was the first one to arrive, for, being possessed of long legs, in spite of his name, he could get over ground at a prodigious rate, given cause. And judging from his ashen face, he had plenty of that right now.

"What is it?" demanded Paul, as the other came panting along.

"Wild man!" gasped Little Billie.

"Whee!" exclaimed Bobolink, who had managed to get near enough to catch what was said.

"'Fraid he nabbed poor Jud!" said Gusty, now reaching the spot, and just about at his last gasp.

"Not much he didn't, because there he comes now!" ejaculated Bobolink.

"Oh! mercy!" exclaimed Little Billie, evidently thinking he meant the wild man.

"It's Jud, and all to the good; but even he looks white around the gills, too, Paul. They must have seen *something*, to give 'em all such a scare," Bobolink went on to say.

"You just bet we did; ask Jud!" declared Gusty, just as though he imagined the others might question their veracity, but would believe the patrol leader, who was now coming along with great leaps and bounds.

And presently Jud Elderkin halted at the group. He looked first at Gusty, and then at Little Billie. There was a question in his eye.

"Sure, we saw it, too, Jud!" declared Gusty, holding up his quivering hand just as though he were in the witness box; but then, as his father was a lawyer, possibly Gusty often experimented on himself, since he meant to either take up the same pursuit in life, or give his magnificent voice a chance to earn him a living in the role of an auctioneer.

"Me too; and say, wasn't it a terror, though?" the tall scout declared.

"Well, I didn't wait long enough to have any words with the Thing," admitted Jud. "You see, I happened to be further away from home than the other fellows, and I knew I'd have more space to cover. So, after letting out a yell to sort of warn 'em, why I just put for cover. Never ran faster even between bases. Thought he'd get me sure before I rounded that bend; but when I looked back, blessed if he wasn't grabbin' up our strings of fish like fun, and making off with 'em. I don't know right now whether I'm just scared, or only boiling mad. Tell me, somebody!"

"A little of both, I guess!" declared Bobolink, grinning.

"Say, then, it wasn't just a big yarn about that wild man, after all; was it?" said Tom Betts.

"How about that, Little Billie; did you see him?" demanded Jud.

"Did I? Think I was runnin' for my health? Why, he looked all of seven feet high to me, and covered with long hair. Talk about your Robinson Crusoe making him a coat of an old nanny goat, that feller was in the same class; eh, Gusty?" loudly asserted the tall boy.

"I saw him, all right, don't you forget it," declared the one addressed. "And I certain sure thought he was after *me*. But if Jud says he took our nice string of bass, why that changes the thing, and makes me mad as hops. Think of us workin' all that time, only to fill up a crazy crank. Next time I go fishin' I'm meanin' to sit home, and do it off the door step."

Paul was revolving many things in his mind and trying to understand.

"I want several of you to go back with me," he said, presently; "the rest head for camp or go about whatever you were doing."

"Want to take a squint at his tracks; eh, Paul?" asked Jud.

"No harm done if we do," remarked Bobolink, thus declaring his intention of being one of those who were to accompany the leader.

Jack also went along, and Jud, making four in all; but the last mentioned refused to budge a foot until he had obtained a healthy-looking club, which he tucked under his arm.

"Now, I want to warn that same critter to keep his distance from me," Jud said, as he led off with long strides. "He gave me one scare, and I promise you that if he tries that game again there's going to be a warm time around these regions. But I reckon he's satisfied with all our nice fish, and we won't see anything of him until he gets good and hungry again. Wonder if he eats 'em raw, Chinese fashion, or has some way of making a fire?"

"What's that over yonder?" asked Paul.

"Where?" gasped Jud, brandishing his club.

"Looks like a string of fish; and so, you see, the wild man didn't get *all* you fellows caught. We'll just pick that lot up, and trot along," observed Paul.

"He got mine, all right; these must have been what one of the other fellows had. You see, they were so badly rattled they just cut and run, and held on to their rods only. Yep, there's a second string of fish, and that accounts for both; but you needn't think mine'll be laying around, for he got 'em.

"Well, show me just about where he was when you saw him last," Paul demanded.

Jud could easily do this. They found the print of human feet in the earth. It must have been an unusually large foot that made the marks; and this tallied with what had been said about the height of the wild man.

"You're not goin' to try and follow him, I hope, Paul?" asked Jud, uneasily, as if he drew the line at certain things, ready and willing as he might be to back the scout master in most ventures.

"Oh! it wouldn't pay us," retorted Paul. "As one of the boys said, we haven't lost any wild man; and so far as I know there's no one missing around Stanhope, so it can't be some man from there. I think we'd do well to mind our own business in this affair; don't you, fellows?"

"Yes, I do," replied Jack, "but I was wondering whether this thing will crop up to give us a heap of bother while we're camping up here."

"How's that?" asked Bobolink. "There's only one thing that gives me any carking care, and you know what that is, Jack, old boy. If I only knew about those boxes, I'd be so much easier in my mind."

"Well," said Paul, "if this crazy man would steal our fish, he'd just as lief take anything else we've got that's good to eat. When he smells our coffee cooking it'll call up some long-forgotten craving for the Java bean; and first thing you know he'll be invading our camp every night, hunting around for any old thing he can steal."

"Now, I like that," said Bobolink, satirically. "Nice prospect, ain't it, not to be able to step out of the tent of nights, without bumping noses with that awful Man Friday in wild animal shows? P'raps in self-defense we may have to do that grand capture act after all, Paul."

"Well, there's nothing more to learn here, so we might as well turn back again. As I don't see anything of your string of fish, Jud, I calculate that he must have gotten away with 'em. We can add a few more to these, and have enough for a regular feast. Come on, boys, back to camp for us."

Some way or other it was noticed that during the early afternoon most of the boys hung around the camp. It seemed to have an especial attraction for them all. One busied himself sorting over the collection of the morning in the way of plants. A second was polishing up certain specimens of quartz he had found, after cracking some of the round stones that had washed on the island during a flood, possibly many years back. A third developed his pictures, having brought along his daylight tank.

And so it went, until Paul smiled to observe what a busy

colony he had in his charge. On his part, he took a rod and line, with some bait, and went off with Jack to add to the number of fish, so that there would be enough for all at supper time. And as the others had fished in one direction, Paul and his chum decided to move in the other.

They put in an hour with very fair success, considering that it was not the best part of the day for fishing.

Of course, as they walked along, keeping close to one another, occasionally Paul and Jack would chat on various subjects. They also kept their eyes open, not wishing to be taken by surprise, should that hairy individual, who seemed to have a craving for fish, rush out at them.

And more than that, Paul had copied the example set by Jud. It was fashionable about that time not to walk forth without a nice little Irish shillelah under one's arm, with which a head could be made to sing unmercifully, in case of necessity.

Paul had just had a pretty lively time with a good fish, and had succeeded in bringing his prize to land, when he happened to look down at the beach on which he was standing. Bobolink and Tom Betts were coming along, as though curious to see how fast the stock of provisions for supper was increasing.

So Paul bent down to examine something that had caught his attention. The other three coming up, Jack having joined Bobolink and Tom, found the scout master still on his hands and knees.

"Hello! found something, have you?" asked Bobolink.

"Mebbe the footprints of the ghost!" chuckled Tom, meaning to be humorous.

But Jack saw that his chum was very serious; and as he dropped down beside Paul, he let his eyes fall upon the sand.

"What's this, Paul?" he remarked, immediately. "Looks like the prow of a rowboat had been pulled up here - why, that's a dead certainty, because look at the plain prints of boots here, and several different kinds, too. Shows that somebody landed here on the island; and Paul, it must have been *after* that rain storm, for these marks don't seem to be washed, as they would be if the rain had beat down on them. What in the world d'ye suppose it means? Are there people on this queer old Cedar Island? If there are, who can they be, and why should they hide from everybody like this?"

As Jack said this he looked up. Bobolink and Tom were staring at the plain marks in the sand, with wonderment written on their faces; and even Paul shook his head.

CHAPTER XIV

TRYING TO FIGURE IT ALL OUT

"We'll have to look into this thing," said Paul, finally, seeing that his three chums were waiting for an opinion from the one they looked up to as their leader.

"But what I said was pretty close to the truth; wasn't it, Paul?" Jack asked.

"Every word of it" came the ready response, for Paul was always willing to give every fellow his meed of praise. "The only trouble is, it stops right where you left off. None of us can say a word after that."

"How many men were there in the crowd?" asked Tom Betts.

"I could make out four," replied Jack; "you take another look, Paul, and see if that's correct."

"I know it is," remarked the scout master, nodding, "because I counted them before I called you. And they seemed to lift something heavy from the boat, which they carried away into the bushes here."

"Whee! something heavy, eh?" burst out the impetuous Bobolink; "and they carried it between them, two and two; was it, Paul?"

"Why, yes, two on each side; if you look close, you can see where they stepped into each other's footprints," assented the patrol leader.

"That's so," agreed Bobolink, after bending down hastily; "just like - er - you've seen the pall-bearers at a funeral!"

"Oh!" exclaimed Tom, turning a little white at the idea.

"Of course, that isn't saying it *was* a funeral," remarked Bobolink, hastily, as he noticed that Paul glanced at Jack, and the two shook their heads a trifle, as though the idea failed to impress them favorably. "But whatever it was, they seemed to find it heavy, the way their toes dug into the sand here."

"Yes, it was heavy, all right," admitted Paul. "I think, from the way the rear men stepped into the prints of the one up head, that whatever they were carrying could not have been very lengthy; in fact, it must have been short, but rather broad."

"Well, that's a smart idea of yours, Paul, and I c'n see how you hit on it," Bobolink was quick to say, with a look of sincere admiration.

"But whatever do you reckon would bring four men up here to this lonely island, carrying some heavy object in a rowboat?" Tom Betts went on.

"That's where we have to do our guessing," Paul replied. "We don't know; and as they haven't been obliging enough to write it out, and fasten the card to a tree, why, we've just got to put on our thinking caps, as my mother would say."

"Well, we've had some experience in the past with hoboes; think they could be a batch of Weary Willies, Paul?" remarked Tom Betts.

"I'm not ready to say off-hand that they're not," replied the other, slowly; "but it hardly seems likely. In the first place, every one of them seemed to be wearing sound shoes. Did you ever know four tramps to do that?"

"Well, I should say not," replied Bobolink, scornfully. "It'd be a wonder if one out of four had shoes that'd hold on without a lot of rope. You clinched that idea the first thing, Paul."

"Then what'd you say they were?" demanded Tom.

Bobolink rubbed his chin reflectively.

"A heap of difference between plain tramps, and the kind they call yeggs; isn't there, Paul?" he asked, presently.

"Everybody says so," came the answer. "Yegg-men are supposed to be the toughest members of the tramp tribe. They're really burglars or safe-blowers, who pretend to be hoboes so they can prowl around country towns, looking up easy snaps about the banks and stores that ought to be good picking. And so you think these four men might belong to that crowd, do you, Bobolink?"

"It's barely possible, anyhow," the one addressed went on, doggedly. "And I was just trying to remember if I'd heard of any robbery lately. There was a store broke into over at Marshall two weeks ago, and the thieves carried off a lot of stuff. But seems to me, the men got nabbed later on. I'm a little hazy about it, though. But supposin' now, that these four men had made a rich haul somewhere, and wanted to hide their stuff in a good place, could they find a better one than up here on Cedar Island?"

The other three exchanged glances.

"I guess that's about right," admitted Tom.

"It's certainly quiet enough to suit anybody; and chances are they wouldn't be disturbed in a coon's age," declared Jack. "Our coming here was a freak. It mightn't happen again in many years."

"And this old island's already got a bad name; hasn't it?" Bobolink went on.

"That would help keep people away," admitted Paul. "I've heard of men coming up in this region winters, trapping the muskrats that swarm in the marshes; but up to cranberry picking time it's almost deserted."

"Jack, you must have had an idea, too?" remarked Bobolink.

"Well, I did; but perhaps the rest of you'll only give me the laugh if I mention it," replied Jack.

"All the same, it isn't fair to keep anything back," Tom declared. "My guess didn't pan out much, and you couldn't have worse luck than that. So tell us."

"Yes, go on, Jack, and give us the benefit of your think-box. I've known you to get away up head more'n a few times, when it came to a live race. And mebbe some of the rest of us mightn't think so badly of your idea as you do yourself," and as he said this Bobolink sat down on the sand to listen, all the while eyeing those mysterious tracks as though he half expected them to give tongue, and tell the true story of their origin.

"Oh! well, that seems only fair, so here goes," Jack began. "Somehow I happened to remember that once on a time I read about some counterfeiters who had their nest in an old haunted mill, away up in the country."

"Whee!" Bobolink said, sitting bolt upright.

"None of the country people would ever go near the place, you see; and when a light happened to be seen in it at night time, they talked about the ghost walking, and all that," Jack continued.

"Huh! that must have been when the boss was paying off his hands," chuckled Bobolink. "I always heard that was the time the ghost walked."

"In this case the truth was only found out by some accident," Jack went on to say, without paying any heed to the interruption. "I think a hunter was overtaken by darkness, having lost himself in the woods. He was a stranger, and had never heard about the haunted mill. So, seeing a light, he went up to ask his way, or if he could get a chance of a bed that night, I forget which. He saw enough to give him a suspicion; and when he did get back to the tavern he was stopping at, he sent word to the Government authorities. A raid resulted, and they caught four counterfeiters hard at work."

"*Four*, you said, Jack!" echoed Tom.

"Yes, just the same number there seems to be here; but then that's only a coincidence, because those others are serving ten-year sentences in the penitentiary. Now, you see, I guess the fact of Cedar Island being said to have a real ghost got me into the idea of thinking about that story I read in the paper. Of course it's a silly idea all around."

"Well, I don't know," said Paul, slowly.

"You don't mean to say you think it might happen that way here?" demanded Jack, seeming to be the only one desirous of "shooting holes" in the proposition he had himself advanced, as Bobolink expressed it later on.

"It's possible," Paul said, simply.

"Huh! for my part," spoke up Bobolink, "I think it's more than that, even. If you asked me straight now, I'd be inclined to say it's probable."

"Same here," remarked Tom Betts, eagerly.

Jack laughed as if pleased.

"I declare, I really expected to hear you knock my idea all to flinders," he remarked.

"But what under the sun could they be carrying in that big box?" asked Tom Betts.

"Box!" muttered Bobolink, frowning, as though the word recalled to his mind a matter that had been puzzling him greatly of late; but he did not think to say anything further on that subject.

"Well, sometimes machinery comes that way," suggested Paul. "If these strange men did turn out to be what Jack said, they might be getting a press of some kind up here, to do their printing with. I never saw an outfit, but seems to me they must have such a thing, to make the bogus bills."

"That's right," added Tom. "I read all about it not long ago. Wallace Carberry's so interested in everything about books and printing, that he clips all sorts of articles. And this one described a kind of press that had been taken in a raid on some bogus money-makers. Yep, it must have been machinery they were lugging off here. Whew! just to think of us bein' mixed up in such a business. I wonder, now, if the Government ever pays a reward for information about such things."

"Oh! rats! that's the last thing a scout should bother his head about," said Bobolink, scornfully. "He ought to see his duty, and do it. Though, of course, if a nice little present happens along afterwards, why, I guess there's no law against a scout acceptin' it; eh, Paul?"

"Certainly not," replied the other, "you've got the idea down pretty fine, Bobolink. But let's see if we can guess anything else. Then we'd better go back to camp, and start the rest of the fellows thinking about it. Perhaps Jud or Andy or Nuthin might dig up something that never occurred to any of us."

But although they talked it over for some little time they did not seem able to conjure up any new idea; everything advanced proved to hinge upon one of the explanations already spoken of. And in the end they were forced to admit that they had apparently exhausted the subject.

"Let's pick up our fish, and stroll back, fellows," proposed Paul, finally.

"Lucky to have any fish, with that hog around," remarked Bobolink.

"Now you're meaning the wild man, I take it?" said Jack.

"No other; the fellow that drops in on you when you ain't expectin' company, and just swipes your string of fish like he did Jud's. I might 'a thought Jud was giving us a yarn to explain why he didn't have anything to show for his morning's work; but both Little Billie and Gusty saw the same thing. Say, that's another link we got to straighten out. What's a crazy man doing up here; and is he in the same bunch that made these tracks?"

"That's something we don't know," admitted Paul.

"But we mean to find out," asserted Bobolink, with a determined snapping of his jaws.

"Perhaps so - anyhow, we'll make a brave try for it," Paul declared.

"He wasn't one of these four, that's flat," said Tom Betts. "We all saw what a big foot the wild man had; and besides, he goes without shoes."

"Glad to see you noticed all that," commented Paul, who always felt pleased when any of the troop exhibited powers of observation, since it proved that the lessons he was endeavoring to impress upon their minds had taken root.

They turned their faces toward the camp, and Paul made sure to pick up the fish he and Jack had caught.

"With what we'e already cleaned, they'll make a fine mess for the crowd," he remarked, pointing out an unusually big fellow that had given him all the fun he wanted, before consenting to be dragged ashore.

"I notice that you both kill your fish as you get 'em," remarked Tom.

"I wouldn't think of doing anything else," replied Jack. "It only takes a smart rap with a club on the head to end their sufferings. I'd hate to think of even a fish dying by inches, and flapping all over the boat or the ground, as it gasps its life away. That's one of the things scouts are taught - to be humane sportsmen, giving the game a chance, whether fish, flesh or fowl, and not inflicting any unnecessary suffering."

"Wonder if anything's happened in camp since we came away; because Bobolink and I have been gone nearly an hour," remarked Tom Betts, to change the subject; for his conscience reproved him with regard to the matter Jack was speaking about.

"What makes you think that?" asked Paul, suspiciously.

"Oh! nothing; only things seem to be on the jump with us right now; and a fellow can't turn around without bumping into a wild man, or some bogus money-makers, it seems. P'raps the ghost'll show up next. Listen! wasn't that somebody trying to blow your bugle, Bobolink, that you left hung up in the tent?"

"It sure was, for a fact. Let's start on a run, fellows. Mebbe they've gone and grabbed that wild man! P'raps he was bent on carryin' off the whole outfit this time. You never can tell what a crazy man'll do next; that's the hard part of being a keeper in a queer house, where they keep a lot of that kind; anyhow a man told me that once who'd been there. But listen to that scout trying to sound the recall, would you? Whoop her up, boys; there's *something* happened, as sure as you live!"

CHAPTER XV

ORDERED OFF

It was about four o'clock in the afternoon of this, the first day of their intended stay on Cedar Island, when Paul and his three comrades came running around the bend of the shore above the camp, and saw some of the scouts beckoning wildly to them.

"They've gone and grabbed him, sure as shooting!" gasped Bobolink, exultantly.

But Jack and Paul noted that while there teemed to be a cluster of the boys no strange form could be seen among them. In fact, they appeared to be greatly excited over something Jud Elderkin was holding.

And in this manner then did the quartette reach the camp.

"Where is he; got him tied up good and hard?" demanded Bobolink, speaking with difficulty, from lack of breath.

Nobody paid the slightest attention to what he was saying; and so Bobolink, happening to notice that it was Curly Baxter who had been taking liberties with his precious bugle, quietly possessed himself of it, and examined it carefully, to make sure that it had not been dented.

"Take a look at this, Paul," said Jud, as he held out the

fluttering piece of paper that had evidently caused all the excitement.

Written upon this the scout master saw only a few words, but they possessed considerable significance, when viewed in the light of the strange happenings of the recent past.

"Leave this island at once!"

Just five words in all. Whoever wrote that order must be a man who did not believe in wasting anything. There was no penalty attached, and they were at liberty to believe anything they chose; just the plain command to get out, and somehow it seemed more impressive because of its brevity.

Paul looked at Jack, and then around at the anxious faces of the other scouts. He saw only blank ignorance there. Nobody could imagine what this strange order meant. The island might have an owner, but at the best it was only a worthless bit of property, and their camping on its shore for a week could not be considered in the light of trespass.

"Where did you get this, Jud?" asked the scout master.

"Why, Old Dan Tucker brought it to me," replied the leader of the Gray Fox Patrol, promptly.

"And where did *you* find it, Dan?" continued Paul, turning on the scout in question, who seemed only too willing to tell all he knew - which, it turned out, was precious little at best.

"Why, you see, I had a dispute with Nuthin about the number of hams fetched on the trip. He vowed there was two, and I said three, countin' the one we'd cut into last night. So to prove it, I just happened to step into the tent where we've got some of the grub piled up. It was three, all right, just as I said. But I found this paper pinned to one of the whole hams, which, you know, are sewed up in covers right from the packers. I couldn't make out what it meant. First I thought

Nuthin was playin' a joke on me; but he denied it. So I took the paper to Jud, seein' that you were away, Paul."

"It was pinned to one of the hams, was it?" asked the scout master, frowning.

"Sure, and the pin's still stickin' in it," answered Dan, positively.

Paul looked around.

"I want to settle one thing right at the start, before we bother any more about this matter," he remarked. "Did any one of you write this, or have you ever seen it before Dan brought it to Jud?"

"He showed it to me," exclaimed Nuthin; "but it was the first time I ever glimpsed that paper or writin', Paul, I give you my word."

"If anybody else has seen it before, I want him to hold up his hand," continued the scout master, knowing how prone boys are to play pranks.

The boys glanced at each other; but not a single hand went up.

"Well, that settles one thing, then," declared Paul. "This note came from some one not belonging to our camp. He must have crawled into the tent from the rear, taking advantage of our being busy. Yes, there's a bunch of scrub close enough to give him more or less shelter, if he crawled on all fours. Let's see if one or two of the tent pins haven't been drawn up."

Followed by the rest, Paul strode over to the tent where a quantity of the provisions were kept. Entering this, he quickly saw that it was exactly as he had suggested. Three of the tent pins, which the boys had pounded down with the camp axe, had been pulled up, and this slack allowed the intruder to crawl under the now loose canvas.

"I can see the place he shuffled along, and where his toes dug into the earth," declared Jack, as he bent over.

"We'll try and follow it up presently, and see where he got on his feet to move off," Paul remarked. "I'd like to find out whether his shoes make a mark anything like some of those we were looking at up the shore, Jack."

"Whew!" exclaimed Bobolink, who was again deeply interested in what was going on, since he had found his precious bugle unharmed.

"Let's look at that paper again," resumed Paul. "The writing was done with a fountain pen, I should say. That seems to tell that the owner was no common hobo. And the writing is as clear as the print in our copybooks at school. The man who did that was a penman, believe me. 'Leave this island at once!' Just like that, short and crisp. Not a threat about what will happen if we don't, you see; we're expected to just imagine all sorts of terrible things, unless we skip out right away. One thing sure, Jud, your wild man never wrote that note, or even pinned it on our ham, because the crawler wore shoes."

"That's right," muttered Jud, his face betraying the admiration he felt for the scout master who knew so well how to patch things together, so that they seemed to be almost as plain as print.

"Now, the rest of you just stay around while I take Jack and Bobolink with me along this trail. We want to settle one thing, and that'll come when we hit the place where this party got up on his feet to move off."

So saying, Paul himself got down and deliberately crawled under the canvas the same way the trespasser had. Jack and Bobolink hastened to follow his example, only too well pleased to be selected to accompany the leader.

It was no great task to follow the marks made by the crawling man. His toes had dug into the soil, going and coming, for apparently he had used the same trail both ways.

"Here we are, boys; now, take a look!" said Paul, presently.

They were by this time in the midst of the timber with which this end of the island was covered. Glimpses of the tents could be seen between the trees; but any intruder might feel himself reasonably justified in rising to his full height when he had made a point so well screened from inquisitive eyes.

This man had done so, at any rate. The plain print of his shoes was visible in a number of places. Both Jack and Bobolink gave utterance to exclamations as soon as they saw these.

"One of the four, that's dead sure!" the former declared, positively.

"I'll be badgered if it ain't!" muttered Bobolink, staring at the tracks.

"So you see, we've settled one thing right at the start," said Paul.

"That's what we have," observed Bobolink. "It's those fellows who carried the heavy load from the rowboat, after landin' on the island, after the rain storm, that want our room more'n our company. The nerve of that bunch to tell us to clear out, when chances are we've got just as much right here as they have - p'raps a heap sight more."

"That doesn't sound much like you wanted to make a change of base, Bobolink?" remarked Paul, smiling.

"No more do I," quickly replied the other. "I'm not used to bein' ordered around as if I was a slave. What if there are four of them, aren't eighteen husky scouts equal to such a crowd? No, siree, if you left it to me, I'd say stick it out till the last horn blows. Give 'em the defi right from the shoulder. Tell 'em to go hang, for all we care. We c'n take care of ourselves, mebbe; and mind our own business in the bargain."

"But it's something else that makes you want to stay?" Paul suggested.

"How well you know my cut, Paul," declared the other. "You reckon I never can stand a mystery. It gets on my nerves, keeps me awake nights, and plays hob with my think-box all the time. Now, there was those boxes - but I guess I'll try and forget all about that matter now, because we've got a sure enough puzzle to solve right on our hands. Who are these four men; what are they hiding on Cedar Island for; why should they want to chase us away if they weren't afraid we'd find out *somethin'* they're a-doin' here, that ain't just accordin' to the law?"

"You've got it pretty straight, Bobolink," admitted Paul. "But since we've learned all we wanted to find out, suppose we go back to the rest of the boys. We must talk this thing over, and decide what's to be done."

"Do you mean about skipping out, Paul?" Bobolink exclaimed. "Oh! I hope now, you won't do anything like that. I'd feel dreadfully mean to sneak away. Always did hate to see a cur dog do that, with his tail between his legs."

"Still, it might seem best to leave here by dark," said Paul.

Something in his manner gave Jack a clue as to the meaning back of these words. He knew the scout master better than did any other fellow in the troop, and was accustomed to reading his motives in his look or manner.

"I take it that means we might *pretend* to clear out, and come back under cover of the night, to make another camp; eh, Paul?" Jack now remarked, insinuatingly.

"That was what I had in mind," admitted the other; "but of

course it'll be up to the boys to settle such a question. I believe in every fellow having a voice in things that have to do with the general business of the camp. But majority rules when once the vote is taken - stay, or go for good."

"Glad to hear you say so," ventured Bobolink. "Because here's three votes that will be cast for sticking it out; and if I know anything about Jud and Nuthin and Bluff, together with several more, the majority will want to stick. But I mean to give them a hint that we think that way. Several weak-kneed brothers are always ready to vote the way the leaders do. When the scout master takes snuff they start to sneezing right away."

"And for that very reason, Bobolink, I don't want you to say a word in advance to any of the fellows. When we have a vote, it should be the free opinion of every scout, without his being influenced by another. But what do you think of the idea, Jack?"

"I think it's just great," answered his chum. "And by the way, if we should conclude to come back to the island again in the night, I know the finest kind of a place where we could hide the motorboats."

"Where is that?" asked the scout master, quickly.

"You haven't been around on the side of the island where the shore curves into a little bay, like. The trees grow so close that their branches overhang the water. If the boats were left in there, and some green stuff drawn around them, I don't believe they'd ever be noticed, unless some one was hunting every foot of the island over for them."

"Yes, I think I know where you mean," said Paul. "I wasn't down by the little inlet you speak of; but back on the shore there's a dandy place among the rocks and trees, where we could pitch a new camp, and keep pretty well hidden, unless we happened to make a lot of noise, which we won't do if we can help it But everything depends on how the boys look at it."

"Anyhow," said Bobolink, resolutely; "I feel that we ought to put it up to them that way; tell 'em how easy it will be to screen the boats, and have a hidden camp. You'll let me tell about that, Paul, I hope, even if I mustn't say you mean to vote to come back?"

"I suppose that would be fair enough, because we ought to hold up our side of the question," the scout master replied, as they drew near the place where the three tents stood, and several groups of chattering scouts could be seen, doubtless earnestly discussing this mysterious thing that had come about; for, of course, Tom Betts had already told all about the suspicious tracks of the four men who had carried a heavy burden into the brush.

They looked eagerly toward the advancing three, as though expecting that Paul would now take them fully into his confidence.

This he proceeded to do without further delay; and it was worth while observing the various shades of emotion that flitted across the faces of the listeners while the scout master was talking. Some seemed alarmed, others disposed to be provoked, while not a few, Bobolink noted with secret glee, allowed a frown to mark their foreheads, as though they were growing angry at being so summarily ordered off the island by these unknown men, who did not even have the decency to present their command of dismissal in person.

He knew these fellows could be counted on to vote the right way when the question came up as to what they should do.

When the entire thing had been explained, so that they all understood it, Paul asked for a vote as to whether they clear out altogether, or appear to do so, only to come back again.

And, just as the sanguine Bobolink had expected, it resulted in thirteen declaring it to be their idea that they should come back, and try to find out what all these queer goings-on meant.

When the result of the vote was made known, even the five who had voted to go moved that it be made unanimous.

Perhaps they came to the conclusion that since a return was decided on it would be safer to be with the rest on the haunted island, than off by themselves in a lone tent on the distant shore, where no assistance could reach them.

"Well, we'd better have an early supper, then, and get away; or since it is getting dark now, perhaps we'll have to put off the eating part until later," Paul suggested.

"Any old time will do for that," declared Bobolink, carelessly, whereupon Old Dan Tucker gave him a look of dismay, and sadly shook his head, as though he did not indorse such a foolish theory at all.

So, when the others were carrying things to the boats, and showing considerable nervousness while doing it, Old Dan managed to fill his pockets with crackers, which he hoped might stave off starvation for a little while at least.

Acting on the suggestion of Jack, the scouts gave all sorts of exhibitions of alarm as they busied themselves taking down the tents, and loading their traps aboard the two motorboats. Every now and then one of them would point somewhere up or down the shore, as though he thought he saw signs of the enemy coming, whereupon a knot of the boys would gather, and stare, and then scatter, to work more feverishly than ever.

They really enjoyed acting the part, too. It seemed to appeal to their fondness for a joke. And the best of it was, they always fancied that somewhere or other at least one pair of hostile eyes must be observing these signs of panic with satisfaction.

Just as darkness began to creep over water and island, clouds shutting out the moonlight again, all was pronounced ready. And then the cheery "chug" of the motors sounded, for the boys purposely made all the noise they could, under the impression that it might seem to add to the appearance of a hasty flight.

In this manner did the troop of scouts break camp before they had been on Cedar Island more than twenty-four hours; and, so far as appearances went, deserted the place of the evil name for good and all.

CHAPTER XVI

UNDER COVER OF DARKNESS

Paul had settled it all in his mind as to what their course should be. He drew a mental map of the island, and its surroundings; and also remembered certain conclusions he had previously entertained connected with the depth of water on all sides, between their late
camp and the mainland.

So the *Comfort* set the pace, which was not very fast; for they wanted darkness to settle fully over the lake, in order that they might move around without being seen from the island.

"Tell me when the island is out of sight, Jud," remarked Paul; for some of the time the two boats were side by side, and nothing interfered with a clear view in the rear.

"Why, it's swallowed up already in the night mist; I can just make out that old cedar that stands on top of the little hill," came Jud's reply.

"Good. Then we'll have an easy time slipping back, I reckon," said Paul.

"Going all the way over to the shore; are you?" asked the other.

"Might as well; though we'll have to feel our way. Pretty shallow; ain't it, Jud?" for the scout master had set the other to work sounding with one of the setting poles, by dropping it over every little while.

"Touch bottom every time but seems to be plenty of water. Guess this lake ain't near so deep as that other one up by Rattlesnake Mountain," Jud remarked.

"Oh! it's many times deeper on the other side of the island," observed Paul. "I picked out this way across for a good reason."

"I suppose you did," Jud said, with a sublime confidence that was refreshing.

"Because, you see," added Paul, "when we start back again, we'll have to do without the help of our motors, for, muffle them as we might, they'd make enough noise to betray us."

"Oh! I see now," declared Jud, chuckling. "In place of the motor business we'll use good hard muscle with these setting poles. And so long as we can touch bottom right along, it ain't going to be a very hard job getting back to the island. You don't think it's more'n half a mile; do you, Paul?"

"Not much more, and we can take our time, Jud. The one thing above all others we've got to keep in mind is silence. Nobody ought to knock a pole against the side of a boat under penalty of being given black marks. And as for talking, it'll have to be in whispers, when at all."

"S-s-sounds g-g-good to m-m-me," said Bluff, who somehow seemed to have gone back to his old stuttering ways; though it might be the excitement that caused the lapse.

Nothing more was said on the way over, though doubtless the boys kept up considerable thinking. They were tremendously worked up over the situation. This scheme proposed by the scout leader seemed to appeal to the spirit of adventure which nearly every boy who has red blood in his veins feels to be a part of his nature.

There was one among them, however, who was silent because of another reason; for Old Dan Tucker always declared it a very bad and injurious plan to try and converse when one's mouth was crammed full; and crackers, too, being apt to get in the wind-pipe, may do all manner of choking stunts. So he said never a word.

They presently could see the other shore looming up, though it was getting very dark, just as though a storm might be threatening to again demoralize them.

"Getting more shoal, Paul," warned the pole heaver.

"How much water have you now?" demanded the leader, ready to give the signal for bringing both motorboats to a stop, when it seemed necessary.

"Eight feet, last time; now it's about seven, short," announced Jud.

"Keep on sounding, and when it gets down to three, let me know," ordered Paul.

They were creeping along at a snail's pace now, so even should either boat strike mud bottom, which Jud had declared it to be, no particular damage would result.

The shore was very close, and still Jud admitted that there was plenty of water.

"Keeps up in great shape, Commodore," he remarked, "reckon we could go ashore here if we felt that way."

"Which we don't," declared Gusty Bellows, in a low tone.

And not a single voice was raised in favor of such a proceeding; if there were any timid souls present, they failed to exhibit their weakness, either through fear of boyish ridicule, or some other reason.

Then Paul shut off power, and when he no longer heard the sound of the *Comfort's* exhaust, Jack followed suit.

"We'll hang out here for half an hour, and then head back," explained Paul.

"The outlet isn't far away from here; is it?" Joe Clausin asked.

"Not very far - on the right," Paul replied. "I had that in mind when choosing to come this way. You see, if we were intending to only go ashore, they'd expect to see a fire burning somewhere. As it is, they'll be sure to think we've dropped down into the Radway, preferring to risk all sorts of danger from the rocks and snags there, rather than stay here another night."

"Makes me think of Napoleon's retreat from Moscow," remarked Nat Smith in the other motorboat.

"Oh! come off, will you?" ridiculed Bobolink. "Napoleon was a good one, but not in the same class with *us*. He never came back, like we're going to do. This retreat is only a fine piece of strategy, remember, while his was in deadly earnest."

They talked in low tones that were cousins to whispers, and certainly could not be heard half way over to the mysterious island, even though water does make the finest conductor of sound possible, as every boy knows.

Finally, when about half an hour had gone, Paul said it was time to make a fresh start. He had thought it all out, and while taking one pole himself, asked the expert, Jud, to handle the other in their boat.

Jack and Tom Betts were to look after those in the *Speedwell*; for the scout master knew that Tom could be very careful, given a job that required caution.

They took their time, and by degrees Paul led the way across the shallow part of the lake. Bobolink had aptly described their movement, when he said it reminded him of the words in the song: "He came right in, and turned around and walked right out again."

Now it was so dark that most of the scouts found themselves confused as to their bearings, the minute they lost sight of the trees along the shore. Some wondered how Paul was going to go straight back over their recent course, when he did not have even the stars to guide him.

But then, there were many other things he did have, one of which was the slight breeze that blew in his face, and which had been directly behind them at the time they left the island.

Slowly and laboriously, in comparison with their other trip, the scouts crossed the stretch of water. And when finally those who were so eagerly watching out for that cedar on the top of the little elevation in the middle of the island whispered to Paul that it was dead ahead, they realized with wonder that the pilot had led them in a direct line back over their course.

Now they altered the line of advance a little. This was in order to approach the island about the place where the little bay extended into its side, as described by Jack. And Paul allowed the other to take the lead, since Jack would be more familiar with the locality than he himself might feel.

Noiselessly did the two boats enter that miniature bay, and glide along until close to the bank, where the overhanging trees afforded the protection they wanted, in order to conceal the craft.

Landing was next in order, and then all their things must again be taken ashore, from tents and blankets, to cooking kettles and eatables.

By now the scouts had reduced many of these things to a system. Every boy knew just what was expected of him; and presently there was a procession of burden bearers carrying things into the brush along a certain trail, once in a while perhaps stumbling a little, but keeping strict silence.

They seemed to enjoy it hugely, too. Their nerves tingled while carrying out this part of the programme - at least, Bobolink said he had such a feeling, and doubtless several more were in the same condition.

Of course there were those who trembled with anticipation of some sudden alarm. And then again, others might be beginning to think they would soon nearly "cave away" with the empty feeling they had; that was what Old Dan Tucker confided in a whisper to Joe Clausin, resting firm in the belief that none of the others knew about the pocket full of crackers, that he called "life preservers" - which, alas, were all gone now, to the last crumb.

Paul led the line and picked out the easiest method of reaching the place he had selected for the new camp among the rocks and trees. It was in a depression, too, the others noticed, when he told them to drop their bundles. That would enable them to have a little fire, since it could not be seen as it would be if they were on a level, or an elevation. And really, a fire was necessary, if Paul meant they should have any supper at all.

"As we brought about all we need, there's no use of making another trip to the boats," Paul remarked in a low tone; from which the others judged that conversation was not going to be entirely cut out, only they must not elevate their voices above a certain pitch, so long as things were as quiet as at present.

Now began the task of getting the three tents in position again. And well had the scouts learned their lesson in this particular; some of them even going so far as to declare that they could do the job with their eyes blindfolded, so familiar were they with every part of the operation.

"Like learning type-writin' by touch in school," Bobolink had said.

After all the tents had been raised, and the blankets placed inside, Paul gave permission for a small cooking fire to be made.

To some boys a fire is always a fire, no matter what its intended use; but the scout who has camped out soon gets to know that there is a vast difference between a camp fire, for instance, and one meant only for getting meals over.

The former may be composed of great logs and branches that send up a cheery and brilliant blaze; but which is next to useless when the cook wants to get close in, and attend to his various kettles and frying pans.

Sometimes a hole is scooped out of the ground, and the fire for cooking made in that, especially when on level ground, and danger exists of hostile eyes discovering the blaze, however small.

As a rule, however, such a fire is made about after this fashion: Two logs may be used, if they have flat surfaces, having been more or less squared off; but when stones can be procured they are to be preferred. Two sides are fashioned out of flat stones, somewhat in the shape of the letter V, only not having the line quite so pronounced. Thus a coffeepot will rest snugly over the smaller end, while the big frying pan cozily covers the larger.

The fire need only be small, but when the cooking commences, there should be for the most part red embers in the fireplace, capable of sending up great heat, with but a minimum of blaze. And there a cook can work in comfort, without dodging back every time a fierce blaze darts toward him, threatening to singe his eyebrows, and shorten his crop of hair.

Jud knew just how to make such a fire, and as they would need several, in order to cook for such a host, some of the other boys busied themselves in copying what he did. They had seen him make such a stone fireplace before, any way, and some of them had practiced the art in private, being desirous of knowing how to do many of the things the leaders were so proficient in.

Soon they had more light, when Jud got his fire started; and it was then that the boys realized just how fitting that spot was for a hidden camp. Their tents could not be seen thirty feet away; and as for the small amount of light made by the three cooking fires, little danger of it being noticed, unless some one were close by, and actually stumbled on the spot.

In fact, the greatest chance they had of being discovered, as Paul well knew, did not come from any sense of sight or hearing, but that of smell. Should the odors from their supper chance to be carried across the island, and in the direction of where these men were staying, they might begin to suspect something was wrong, and start an investigation that would lead to the discovery of the new camp.

But Paul had also noticed that the night breeze was doing them another good service; it had helped him find his way back to the island through the darkness resting on the big lake; and now, blowing toward the distant shore, the odors of cooking coffee, and frying bass would be taken entirely away.

And anyhow, there were eighteen half-starved scouts who had to be fed, come what might. So the cooking went on apace, and in due time supper was announced as ready. At which more than a few of the waiting lads heaved sighs of satisfaction, and Old Dan Tucker, as usual, managed to be the first to sit down.

CHAPTER XVII

PITCHING TENTS IN THE "SINK"

"This thing is giving us lots of good practice at making camp, and that's something," Bobolink remarked while he ate, always taking care to keep his voice down to a low pitch, so it would not carry far on the night air; though for that matter the wind had increased by now and was making quite some noise through the tops of the trees around them.

"I'd like to see anybody put up tents faster and better than we did right here," declared Frank Savage; who had by now about recovered from the feeling of sickness which came so near keeping him at home, when the expedition was formed.

"And as for fires, these couldn't be beat," observed Spider Sexton, as he began to catch glimpses of the bottom of his tin platter, after making away with some of the food that had been piled high on it by the cook of his mess.

"And talk about the grub - it just takes the cake," admitted Old Dan Tucker; though no one seemed to pay the least attention to what he thought, for they knew him of old, and that the present meal was always the "best he had ever eaten, barring none."

Of course it was only natural that while the scouts were enjoying their meal in this fashion, many looks betrayed an uneasiness on the part of some among their number. Possibly they were wondering whether it could be that hostile eyes were fixed upon them then and there, and if so, what those strange, unknown men, who seemed to want to rule the island, would do when they discovered that the scouts had disobeyed their order to leave.

Would they resort to violence? It would not be an easy task to banish a dozen and a half lively boys, they were thinking.

Paul had made up his mind with regard to certain things that must be done. First of all, they ought to get their heads together, and decide on a plan. Should they make any sort of attempt that night to explore the island? He owned a splendid little hand electric torch, into which he had slipped a fresh battery before starting out on the voyage along the two rivers; and this might prove very useful in searching dark and gloomy parts of the island. But on the whole, it seemed so foolish to think of such a thing, Paul wanted the rest to settle the matter.

So, still cautioning them to speak only in whispers at the most, he placed the whole matter before them; much as might the chairman of a meeting, after which he asked in so many words:

"You've heard all I know about it; now, what is your pleasure, fellows?"

"So far as I'm concerned," said Bobolink, always the first to speak; "I'm willing to do anything the rest say, or go wherever they want to head; but to be honest, boys, I'd think we were off our base if we went prowling around this queer old island at night time. There are a heap of things about it that some people don't want us to know, it seems; and we ought to take daylight to spear such facts."

Others were of the same opinion; and when Paul put the vote, it was overwhelmingly the sentiment of the meeting that they simply take things as easy as they could until dawn came, and then, with fourteen hours of light ahead, do all the exploring they liked.

That settled it, since there could be no going behind the returns when a majority favored any move. Accordingly, they made preparations for passing the night as the conditions best allowed.

"Of course, we must have sentries posted to keep watch?" remarked Jack.

"All through the livelong night. They will have to be changed every hour; and four can be on guard at a time. That'll give about two turns to every scout, with a chance to get four hours sleep between times on duty."

And having said his, Paul, as the acting scout master, proceeded to assign each one to his post number. There was no confusion. They had practiced this same movement many a time, and now that it was to be carried out, the boys profited by their experience.

It could be seen that there was a condition of almost feverish excitement under the surface, try as they might to conceal the fact by an appearance of coolness. A real peril seemed to be hovering over them, since they had chosen to disobey the mandate of the unknown who seemed to claim the island as his private property. And if they were discovered during the night, there would be no telling what might happen.

At the same time the boys were enjoying the novel experience. It seemed to give them a peculiar thrill, not unlike that of a daring skater who shoots boldly over thin, new ice, that crackles under him, and bends in a dreadful way, but does not break, because his passage has been too swift.

In the morning Paul would pick out several of them, as he thought best; and with this exploring party set out to learn what the island contained. Meanwhile they would rest quietly in that rocky retreat, in the hope that their return had not been noted by any observing eye, and that their presence on the island was utterly unknown.

The sentries had been selected, and every boy knew just when his turn to take a post would come around. Those who were ready to lie down and get some rest were expected to arouse their successors, so that the thing was calculated to run along as smoothly as though on a greased track.

If anything out of the ordinary came to pass, and there was time to arouse the scout master, Paul wanted it done. He could not remain awake himself more than any one of the others, much as he might wish to be on the job all the time; but that need not prevent his keeping in touch with whatever happened.

Paul still had his shotgun, and had of course made sure to bring it from the motorboat when he led his column of burden-bearers trailing through the timber and rocks to that little sink in which the new camp had been pitched. It had served him often and well, and he was accustomed to placing the utmost confidence in the trusty little weapon. But he hoped he would find no occasion to use it now, and against human beings. Only as the very last resort would he turn to this.

Still, there are times when the presence of an empty gun has done wonders; since imagination invests it with all the attributes of a loaded weapon. And that was one of the many reasons why Paul kept the double-barreled gun close to him, even when he crept into the tent to which he was assigned, and lay down on his blanket to try and get a little sleep.

Some of the other boys whispered for a while, as they lay with their heads close together; but they were too sleepy to keep this up for long; so that one by one they dropped off, until from their regular breathing it was easy to guess that all had surrendered to the heavy hand of sleep.

Those on guard duty were not supposed to move about very much. They had been posted at what might be called the four corners of the camp. Here they could, between them, about cover all the space around the sink, for their positions were on the more elevated ground.

And as the clouds were breaking at the time Paul crawled under the tent, he felt pretty sure that before long they would have the assistance of the moon, now more than half full, and which would not set until after midnight.

Those who were the first on duty fulfilled their part of the programme faithfully. After standing out their "spell," they proceeded to quietly awaken those who were scheduled to follow after them. Each fellow knew who his successor was, and it had been made a part of his duty to see that this scout was not only awakened, but on the job; after which he himself could crawl in under his blanket, and take it easy until his second turn came, hours later.

Thus Bobolink was one of the second watch. In turn he would have the pleasure of arousing the commander, and seeing that Paul took up his duty; for in laying out the schedule Paul had not spared himself in the least.

Bobolink was an imaginative boy. He could see many things that others were apt to pass by without discovering anything out of the ordinary. It was a weakness which Bobolink had to guard against; lest he discover things that had no foundation in fact.

He sat there, listening and looking, for a long time. The music of the breeze in the tree-tops made him a little nervous at first; but presently he seemed to get more accustomed to the sounds, and then they made him drowsy, so that he had to take himself sharply to task more than once because his eyes found it so easy to shut.

Wishing to have something to think about, so as to keep his wits aroused, Bobolink began to try and figure out just where his fellow sentinels were located and imagine what they were doing. Could they be struggling, as he was, to keep awake, one of the hardest things a boy can battle with?

What was that? Surely something moved out yonder among the scrub!

Bobolink sat straight up. He was no longer sleepy. This thing seemed to have made his eyes fly wide open; and with his heart pumping at a tremendous rate, sending the hot blood bounding through his veins, surely he was now in no danger of sleeping on his post.

He watched the spot from which the sound had seemingly come. The moon penetrated the bushes only faintly, because it was now nearing the western horizon, its journey for the night almost done. Strive as Bobolink might to see whether any one was crawling along there, he could not for a time make sure.

Then he detected a movement that must mean something. And at the same time he discovered what seemed to be twin glowworms in the darkness.

Bobolink had had some little experience in such things, and had read a good deal on the subject. He knew that in the night time the eyes of many wild animals, particularly of the cat tribe, can appear luminous, so that, seen in a certain kind of gloom, they seem to be like yellow globes. And that was what these were.

"Huh!" said Bobolink to himself, after he had watched these queer glowing balls of fire move several times, that proved in his mind they must be the eyes of an animal: "Guess I better give Paul the high sign, and let him figure out what it is."

And with that he started to creep into the camp, leaving his post for the time being unguarded; for with three other sentries on duty Bobolink did not imagine there could be any danger in his withdrawing from the line.

CHAPTER XVIII

WHAT LAY IN THE BRUSH

"Wake up, Paul!"

Bobolink accompanied these whispered words by a gentle shake. He seemed to know instinctively just where the scout master was lying; or else it must have been, that all this had been systematically laid out beforehand; and every fellow had a particular place where he was to curl up in his blanket when not on duty.

Paul was awake instantly, even though he had been far gone in sleep at the moment that hand touched his arm.

"All right, Bobolink," he said, in a low tone, so as not to arouse any of the others. "I'm with you. Time up?"

"Not quite, Paul; but there's some sort of beast creeping around the camp; and I thought you ought to know."

Paul sat up at once.

"You did the right thing, Bobolink," he remarked, quietly.

The sentry could hear him groping around, as if for something. Presently Paul seemed to have found what he sought. Of course it was his shotgun.

Wildcats were to be found in some of the woods not many miles from Stanhope. The scouts knew this, because they had experience with these bold pests, who had been attracted by the smell of food in their camp. Besides, there were sometimes packs of wild dogs roaming the woods that might need to be taught a lesson, in case they gave the campers any trouble.

So Paul had been wise to bring that double-barreled gun along. In a pinch it would prove a handy thing to have with them. And no doubt it gave Bobolink considerable satisfaction to realize that Paul had such a weapon handy.

Immediately the sentry started to crawl out of the tent again, with Paul close at his heels. A head was raised, and one of the supposed sleepers watched the dim figures retreating.

It was Nuthin, who had chanced to be restless, and was awake at the time Bobolink came in to arouse the scout master. He had heard all that passed between them, and of course felt a thrill at the idea of some ferocious wild beast prowling around the tents.

Hardly had the other pair withdrawn before Nuthin started after them. He might be a rather timid boy by nature; but when there was anything going on Nuthin could not rest content unless he placed himself in a position where he could see or hear - perhaps both.

Bobolink led the way back to the post he had been occupying at the time he made his discovery. He hoped those luminous eyes would still be there, because it might not look just right should he be able to show no proof of his story; and boys will take occasion to make all sorts of jeering remarks about a fellow falling asleep on his post, and dreaming wonderful things.

So it was with considerable anxiety that the sentry crept along to the very spot which he remembered he had been occupying at the time.

Considerably to his dismay he could see nothing. There was the patch of brush in which he had discovered those gleaming orbs, and from which had arisen a low, threatening growl when he first moved off; but look as he might Bobolink was unable to detect the first sign of a hostile presence.

He felt disgusted with himself. Luck seemed to be playing him all manner of tricks of late, and nothing went right. There was that affair of the queer boxes which had been bothering him so long; then the mystery of the unknown men who had ordered the scouts to leave the island in such a peremptory fashion, without giving the least reason for their churlishness. And now, here, even this little matter could not work straight.

"It's gone, Paul!" he felt compelled to mutter, after striving several times to detect some sign, however faint, of those terrible yellow eyes.

"Just where did you see it, Bobolink?" asked the scout master, knowing from his chum's manner how disappointed the sentry must feel that he was thus unable to prove his assertion.

"Right in that brush yonder; you c'n see it looks darker than anything else," replied Bobolink, eagerly; as if hoping that after all Paul's eyes might prove better than his own, and pick up the lost glow.

"Well, it seems to have gone away, then," said the scout master.

"I'm afraid so," grumbled Bobolink, for all the world as though his whole reputation for veracity depended on his showing the other that he had not been imagining things when he gave his alarm.

"What did you see?" continued Paul.

"Two yellow eyes, and say, weren't they just awful, though? But seems like the varmint has side-stepped, and vamoosed.

Just my luck, hang it! I wanted you to see 'em the worst kind, Paul."

"A pair of shining eyes, eh? When you moved, did you hear anything, Bobolink?"

"Sure I did. It growled just like our dog does at home, when he's got a bone, and anybody gets too near him," the sentry hastened to explain.

"Made you think of a dog, did it, and not a cat?" asked Paul, quickly.

"Why, yes, I reckon it did," replied Bobolink; "leastways, that's what came into my mind. But then a big cat, a regular bobcat, I take it, could growl that way, if it felt a notion to."

"You came straight in to wake me up, of course?" continued Paul, wishing to figure on the time that might have elapsed since Bobolink left his post.

"Crawled right in, and we got back here in a jiffy; but you see it was no use when that jinx is on my trail, meanin' to loco everything I do. Now, I reckon if it'd been any other feller in the bunch, the critter'd just stood its ground, and I'd be vindicated. But me - I'm hoodooed of late, and can't do a thing straight."

"Listen!" said Paul, a little sharply, as though he had no sympathy with such talk.

They strained their hearing for possibly a full minute. Then Bobolink, who liked to talk, could no longer hold in.

"What'd you think you heard, Paul?" he whispered.

"A little rustling sound just alongside the brush you pointed out," the scout master replied.

"But you didn't get it again; did you?" urged the other.

"No. But that needn't be proof that something isn't there, and watching us, even if we don't glimpse his eyes," replied Paul.

"Oh!" ejaculated Bobolink, with a sudden sense of relief in his voice.

"You heard the rustling then; didn't you?" Paul demanded.

"I sure did, and right over back of the brush it seemed to be. P'raps he's givin' the camp the shake, Paul; mebbe he's made up his mind it ain't as healthy a place as he thought, after all."

"It couldn't be one of the other sentries moving around, I suppose?" ventured Paul, at which his companion gave a low chuckle.

"With those glaring yellow eyes? Well, hardly, Paul. My stars! but if you'd only seen 'em, you'd never say that. And besides, the boys were ordered not to leave their posts, only to wake up the fellow that came after 'em. Oh! put it down for me that isn't any of our bunch stirring around."

"Then I must find out what it is!" said Paul, with a ring of determination in his voice.

"Wow! d'ye mean to rush the beast, Paul, and try to knock him over with a charge of Number Sevens?" demanded Bobolink.

"I've got something better than that to scare him off," replied Paul. "You know we don't want to shoot a gun, if we can help it; because the report would tell the men that we'd come back, and might bring trouble. I've got my little electric hand torch with me, and if I flash that into the face of any wild animal the chances are it'll give him a scare that'll send him off about his business."

"Oh! I forgot all about that," said Bobolink. "It's just the thing, too. How lucky you brought it along, Paul."

Bobolink looked on a good many things as "luck," one way or the other, when of a truth they were really planned ahead. The scout master had realized that such a useful little contrivance would be apt to come in handy on many occasions, when camping out, and had made it a particular point to put the torch in his pack before leaving home.

He had it beside him as he slept, but did not consider it wise to press the button when awakened, lest the flash arouse the others who were sleeping in the same tent.

Bobolink could feel him moving away, and not meaning to be left behind, he started after. Bobolink possessed courage, even if he lacked discretion. The possibility of an encounter with this doubtless savage animal did not deter him from following his leader.

Again they heard that suspicious rustling in the bushes ahead, this time louder than before. And quickly on the heels of this sound came a low, threatening growl that, strangely enough, made Bobolink chuckle softly, he was so pleased over having his announcement proven true to the Commodore of the motorboat fleet.

"Look out, Paul," he whispered; "he's laying for you in those bushes. Better keep your gun handy, and be ready to give him Hail Columbia!"

Paul did not answer. He had his gun held in such a way that it could be fired with a second's warning. At the same time his left hand was gripping the little electric torch, with his thumb pressed against the trigger that would connect the battery, and send an intense ray of light wherever he pointed.

When he heard another rustle, and a growl even more vicious than before, he judged about the position of the sounds, and pointing the end of the torch straight ahead, pressed the button.

As the vivid flash followed Paul saw something that looked like a crouching panther staring at the dazzling glow of his torch - a hairy beast that had rather a square head, and a tail that was lashing to and fro, just as he had seen that of a domestic cat move with jerks, when a hostile dog approached too close to suit her ideas of safety.

CHAPTER XIX

LAYING PLANS

"Whee!"

That, of course, was Bobolink giving expression to his feelings when he too saw the crouching figure of the ugly beast in the pile of brush.

He fully expected that Paul would now feel it necessary to raise his gun to his shoulder, and fire, on the spur of the moment. Contrary to his belief, he found that the scout master did nothing of the sort. Instead, Paul took a deliberate step forward, straight toward the animal that lay there, staring at the blinding light.

"Oh I my stars! he's going to scare him off with only that light!" said Bobolink, talking to himself; and yet, strange to say, he followed close at the heels of the advancing scout master, clutching his club tightly, and doubtless fully determined that if they were attacked, he would make the stout weapon give a good account of itself.

For a brief space it seemed an open question whether the animal would turn tail and slink away, or openly attack the advancing boys. But there was evidently something in that approaching dazzling light, and the presence of human beings behind it, that proved too much for the beast. He gave a sudden turn, and bounded off, vanishing in the denser scrub beyond; and for a short time the listening Bobolink could hear the sound of his retreat.

"Whew I that was the stuff, Paul!" cried Bobolink. "He just couldn't look you in the eye; could he? That fierce little staring orb was too much for him. But what was it, Paul, a panther?"

Some one laughed back of them, and turning, light in hand, Paul saw Nuthin.

"What ails you, and how did you get here?" demanded Bobolink.

"Heard what you said to Paul in the tent, and wanted to see what was up, so I just crawled out," answered the smaller scout, still grinning, as though he had discovered something comical in the adventure.

"Well, what ails you?" Bobolink demanded again, feeling irritated somehow.

"Panther! Well, I guess he hasn't got that wild, yet!" ejaculated Nuthin.

Paul began to understand something about it.

"See here, Nuthin," he said, sternly; "you know that was a dog, as well as I do; have you ever seen him before? Do you know him?"

Nuthin laughed softly.

"Guess you fellows must have forgot that old mongrel dog, Lion, we used to have," he went on. "Well, he disappeared a long time ago, and we never knew what did become of him. There always was a sorter wild streak in the critter. And now it seems that he's found, it nicer to live like a wolf in the woods, than stay at home and be tied to a kennel. Because that was Lion, I give you my word for it!"

George A. Warren

"Mebbe he smelled you here, and wanted to make up again?" suggested Bobolink.

"Don't you believe it," retorted Nuthin. "He never did like me, and my dad wouldn't let me go near his kennel. When he skipped out we all felt glad of it. And to think he'd show up here, of all places! What d'ye reckon he's doin' over here on this island, Paul?"

"Listen. When he got away from you did he have a rope around his neck, with six feet of it trailing on the ground?" Paul asked.

"Did he? Not any that I know about. We always kept him fastened with a chain; and when he broke away, it was his collar that busted. I've got it home yet," was the response.

"Well, that dog had the rope, just as I described. He's been tied up, of late, and broke away," the scout master observed, with conviction in his voice.

"Then he must have been in the keep of these men who're doin' somethin' queer over here on Cedar Island, and don't want a parcel of peepin' scouts around; looks that way, don't it, Paul?" Nuthin inquired.

"I was wondering whether it could be that crowd, or the other," Paul replied, musingly.

"D'ye mean the wild man?" asked Bobolink.

"It might be," replied Paul. "If your old dog, Nuthin, has taken to the free life of the woods - gone back to the type of his ancestors, as I've heard of dogs doing many a time - why, you see, he'd just seem to fit in with a wild man who lived about like the savages used to away back."

"Wonder if he'll come again to bother us?" queried Bobolink.

"Honestly now, I don't think he will," Paul made answer. "That little evil eye of the torch threw a scare into him he won't forget in a hurry. I suppose he must have been roaming around, and got a sniff of our cooking. That made him feel hungry, and he was creeping in closer and closer, in hopes of stealing something, when we broke up his game. And now, if it isn't time for me to go on duty, I'll crawl in again, and get a few more winks of sleep."

"Say, Paul, don't you think it'd be about right to leave that little flashlight with me, in case the dog comes around again?" asked Bobolink.

"I was going to say that very same thing; and when my turn comes you can hand it over again. Here you are, Bobolink; and don't go to fooling with it, unless you really hear something."

"I won't, Paul," replied the other. "But chances are, I'd better make the rounds and tell the other fellers about what happened; because they must have seen the flash, and heard us talkin' over here; which will throw 'em into a cold fit, wantin' to know all about it."

"A good idea, Bobolink," observed the other, as he and Nuthin moved toward the tents again.

The balance of the night passed without any further alarm. If the wild dog came prowling around again, attracted by the presence of good things to eat, which may have reminded him of other days when he was content to remain chained up in the Cypher back yard, and take the leavings from his master's table, he certainly did not betray his presence nor could he muster up enough courage to crawl into the camp, when it was guarded by such a terrible flashing eye.

Morning arrived in good time, and the boys were on the alert. This novel experience was having its effect on them all. They showed that their sleep could not have been as sound as appearances might indicate, for many had red eyes, which were the cause of considerable comment, and not a little good-natured chaff on the part of those who betrayed no such telltale signs of wakefulness.

Breakfast was prepared about in the same fashion as the supper had been on the preceding night. Fires were carefully lighted, and such fuel chosen, which, in the opinion of the best judges, would be least apt to send up heavy smoke, such as might betray their presence on the island.

All these little things were supposed to be a part of their education as scouts and woodsmen. They aroused considerable interest among the boys, many of whom had never bothered their heads before to discover that kinds of wood burned in various ways; that one might give out only a light brown smoke, hard to discern, while another would send up a dense smudge that could not fail to attract the eye of any watcher.

Paul showed them that when they wanted to signal with smoke, as all scouts are taught to do when learning the wigwag code, they must be careful to select only this latter kind of wood, since the other would not answer the purpose.

He had been thinking deeply over the matter, and had about made up his mind as to what course they should pursue. Like most of his comrades, Paul was averse to being driven away from Cedar Island by unknown parties, without at least another effort to explore the mysterious place, and making an attempt to discover what sort of business these men were engaged in.

That it was something unlawful he was convinced, as much as any of his chums. Indeed, everything would seem to point that way. Men do not often hide themselves in an unfrequented section of the country, unless they are engaged in some pursuit that will not stand the light of day.

At one time Paul had even suspected that these men might be some species of game poachers, who wishing to defy the law that protected partridges, and all feather and fur-bearing creatures in the woods, during the summer season, had taken up their dwelling on lonely Cedar Island.

This was in the beginning. On thinking it over, however, he came to the conclusion that there was hardly enough game of all kinds within fifty miles of Stanhope to pay several men to spend their time snaring it; and so on this account he had thrown that theory overboard.

As they ate their breakfast the boys talked of nothing else but the mystery of the island, and many were the expressions of opinion that they must not think of leaving without doing everything in their power to lift the curtain.

They wanted to know who the strange men were who had brought some bulky object across from the mainland in a rowboat; what business they were engaged in there; who the wild man might be, and last of all whether he had any connection with the others.

"You see," declared Bobolink, in his customary impressive way of talking, "it looks to me as if they had him here to scare meddlers off. Who wants to rub up against a wild man? Everybody would feel like giving the hairy old fellow a wide berth, believe me. But Paul, if you make up a bunch to explore this bally old island, please let me go along."

There were others just as anxious and then again some gave no expression to indicate how they felt about it. So the wise scout master, not wishing to have any half-hearted recruits with him on such an errand, observed these signs, and made sure to pick only such as had pleaded for recognition.

"You can go along, Bobolink," he said, presently; "and I shall need five others in addition. Jack, you're one; then there's Bluff, Tom Betts, Phil, and Andy. Jud Elderkin will be left in full charge here, and every scout is expected to look to him as the chief while I'm gone. Is that all understood, fellows?"

Everybody looked satisfied - those who had been selected because they wanted to be with the party of exploration and the scouts who would remain behind because they had no particular desire to prowl through that dense undergrowth, looking for what might prove to be a jack-o'-lantern.

And as they continued to devour the food that had been cooked over the little fires they exchanged confidences, all sorts of queer theories and plans being suggested. For when eighteen wide awake scouts put their heads together, it can be set down as positive that little remains unsaid after they have debated any subject pro and con.

CHAPTER XX

THE EXPLORING PARTY

Soon after breakfast was over, Paul began to make his arrangements. Like a wise general he wanted to have all the details arranged beforehand, so far as he could do so.

"I hope you'll take the gun along, Paul," remarked Bobolink, when those who had been selected to accompany the leader were stowing some crackers and cheese in sundry pockets, so that they might have a little lunch, in case they were delayed longer than seemed probable.

"Yes, because we're more apt to find need for it than those who stay in camp," the scout master had replied; which fact seemed to give Bobolink considerable satisfaction.

He had not liked the looks of that big fellow which Nuthin claimed to have recognized as his old Lion. If they chanced to run across the beast again, it might feel disposed to attack them; and nothing would please Bobolink more than to have Paul bowl the creature over with a single shot. Any dog that did not have the sense to stay at home, and feed at the hands of a kind master, deserved to get the limit, he thought.

"It isn't that alone," Bobolink had protested, when Paul took him to task for showing such a bloodthirsty spirit; "I've been hearing lately that some of the farmers up this way are complainin' about dogs killin' their lambs this last spring. And chances are, this same Lion's been one of the pack that did the mischief. Once they start in that way, nothin' can cure 'em but cold lead. My father said that right out at table. So you see, when dogs take to runnin' loose, they're just like boys, an' get into bad ways."

Paul thought this was a pretty good argument. He had himself made up his mind that should they ever meet that animal again, and he showed a disposition to attack any of the scouts, there was only one thing to do.

"How about getting into communication with you while you're gone?" asked Jud, who was naturally feeling the new responsibilities of his position more or less, and wished to be posted.

"It might be found a good thing," replied the scoutmaster; "and we could do it easy enough by flags, if we managed to get to the top of that hill where the lone cedar grows. So all the time we're away, Jud, be sure and have a scout posted in a tree, where he can watch that cedar, keeping his flag handy to answer, if he gets the signal.

"Guess that can be fixed, all right," declared Jud.

"Have him keep his eye out for smoke at the same time," continued Paul. "We might want to tell you something, even without getting up to that cedar tree. And in case you felt like sending back an answer, you'd better have the boys collect a lot of that wood I showed you, that makes a black smoke. You know our smoke code, Jud; no danger of our failing to make good while you're handling the other end of the line."

That made Jud smile, and feel like doing everything in his power to satisfy the scout master. A few drops of oil prevents a vast amount of friction. Paul knew there are few boys who do not like to be appreciated; and they will do double the amount of work if they feel that they possess the full confidence of the one who has been placed in command over them.

When the word was finally given for the little expedition to leave camp, and start into the unknown depths of the island, those who were to remain behind insisted on shaking hands all around, and wishing them the best of luck. Bobolink pretended to make light of it, and to laugh at the fellows.

"Great Scott! you'd think we were going away off to Hudson's Bay, not to come back again for many moons, if ever!" he scoffed. "Talk about Stanley's farewell to Livingstone in the African jungle, why it wasn't in the same class as this. Don't you dare try to embrace me, Dan Tucker. What d'ye think I am, the pretty new girl that's come to town, and who danced with you at our class spread? Hands off, now! And don't any of you cry when we're gone. I declare if you aren't turnin' into a lot of old women."

So the seven scouts strode away from the hidden camp in the sink, plunging into the heavy growth of timber that covered most of the island. Once only did they turn, to wave a goodbye to their watching companions, who flourished their hats in response, but dared not give the cheer that was in their hearts, because Paul had enjoined the strictest silence.

Paul and Jack had more than once tried to figure out what Cedar Island must look like; but at the best it was only guess work. None of them had ever been here before, and so far they had only roamed over a small portion of one end of the island, so that they could not tell even its general shape.

That was one of the reasons why Paul wanted to climb the little hill on which grew the cedar from which the island must have taken its name. Once they gained this point, he fancied they might be able to see all parts of the place, and in this manner get a comprehensive idea as what it was like.

They kept pretty well together as they pushed through the brush and timber. Paul instructed them to watch constantly on all sides, so that nothing might escape their scrutiny; and as the little band of scouts pushed deeper into the unknown depths of the mysterious island, they felt more than ever a sense of the responsibility that rested upon their shoulders.

As one of the boys had remarked before, this was good training. They could look back to other occasions when they had roamed the woods, once in search of a little chap who had been lost; but somehow these incidents lacked the flavor of mystery that surrounded them now.

If these men should turn out to be what they already suspected, lawless counterfeiters, would they not be apt to show a revengeful spirit if the persistent boys interfered with their business to any extent?

Just how far he would be justified in leading his companions on, when there was this element of danger in the affair, was a serious question, which Paul had as yet not settled in his mind. He was waiting until something more definite turned up, and when that occurred he expected to be governed by circumstances to a great extent.

Of course they had frequent little shocks. These came when some small animals rustled the bushes in fleeing before them, or a bird started out of the thick branches of a tree.

The boys were keyed up to such a pitch that their nerves were on edge. When a crow, that had been watching their coming with suspicious eye, gave a series of harsh caws, and flapping his wings, took flight, Andy caught hold of Bluff's sleeve, and gave it a tug.

"Q-q-quit t-t-that!" exclaimed Bluff, in a shrill whisper. "G-g-guess I'm k-k-keyed up enough, without m-m-akin' me j-j-jump out of my s-s-skin!"

"Arrah but I thought it was that ould dog a-goin' to lape at us, so I did!" muttered the Irish lad, shaking his head, and grasping his cudgel more firmly.

All of them had been wise enough to arm themselves in some way before starting out. And when seven fairly muscular boys wield that many clubs, that have been tried and found true, they ought to be capable of doing considerable execution. But in truth there were but six of the cudgels, for Paul carried his gun only.

They had by now cleared quite considerable ground, even though their progress was in anything but a direct line. On account of dense patches of thorn bushes Paul found it necessary to make various detours; but then this did not matter to any great extent; for while it added to the length of their journey, at the same time it promised to reveal more of the island to their search.

One thing surprised Paul. They found the trees so dense that most of the time it was possible to obtain only glimpses of the sky above. Fortunately the sun continued to shine. He thought it must be pretty dingy here on a cloudy day. And the more he saw of Cedar Island the less he wondered that some of the ignorant country people believed it to be haunted.

Bobolink must have been allowing his mind to run in a similar groove, for presently pushing up alongside Paul, he remarked in a whisper:

"Gee! did you ever see a more spooky place than this is, Paul? Now, if a fellow *did* believe in ghosts, which of course I don't, here's where he'd expect to run across some of them. Look at that hollow over yonder, would you? There goes a woodchuck dodging back into his hole in the bank. Ain't it queer how all these animals ever got across from the mainland to this island? Why, seemed like all of half a mile to me."

"Wait till we get on top of that hill, and perhaps the thing won't seem so queer, after all," replied Paul. "I was thinking the same way; and then it struck me that the land might be a whole lot closer to the island on the northern side. Why, how do we know but what it's only a narrow strait there?"

"I wonder, now," mused Bobolink, who always found much food for thought in what information he extracted from the scout master.

They kept on for some five minutes longer, under about the same conditions. Paul, however, began to believe that they must by now be drawing somewhere near the foot of the little hill that arose near the center of the island, as closely as they could figure from their camp at the southern end.

The result of their watchfulness was made apparent when Tom Betts suddenly declared that he had seen something that looked like a blacksmith's forge just beyond a screen of bushes ahead of them.

Cautiously advancing, the seven scouts presently found themselves looking upon the exact object Tom had mentioned, which proved that his powers of observation were good. It was a forge of some sort, with a bellows attached, and a wind screen, but no shelter over the top; which fact would seem to indicate that it must be in the nature of a field smithy, used for certain purposes to heat or melt metal.

There being no sign of life around, Paul and his six followers swarmed out of the brush, and surrounded the forge, which was about as unlikely a thing to be run across, away in this forsaken quarter of the country, as anything they could imagine.

And as Paul examined the portable forge closer he made an interesting discovery.

CHAPTER XXI

A MYSTERY OF THE OPEN GLADE

"This has been used since we had that hard rain, fellows," Paul observed.

Some of the others had noticed him handling the ashes that marked where the fire had been.

"Say, they are not warm, now, are they?" asked Phil, looking uneasily around, as if half expecting to see some rough men come swarming out of the bushes.

"Oh! I didn't mean that," replied the scout master. "But you can see for yourselves that when it rains there's nothing to keep the water from running down over this forge. In that case the ashes would be soaked. If you look again you'll see these are perfectly dry, and have never been wet."

Several of the scouts picked up some of the ashes, and found that it was exactly as Paul stated. They were as dry as powder; and could certainly never have been rained upon.

"That means the forge has been used since the storm that helped us get through that muddy canal of Jackson's Creek; is that what you mean, Paul?" asked Bobolink.

"Nothing else," replied the other, still continuing his investigations, as if he hoped to make some further discovery, that might tell them what the field forge was intended for, when these unknown men carried it to this secluded island.

"Great governor, Paul!"

Bobolink had stooped, and picked something from the ground. This he was now holding in his hand, and staring at it, as though he could hardly believe his eyes.

The other scouts crowded around him, and their eyes, too, widened when they discovered what it was.

"A quarter of a dollar!" exclaimed Jack.

"And a shining new one in the bargain," declared Tom Betts.

"What d'ye think of that, now?" said Phil.

Paul reached over, and took possession of the coin.

"Did you find that, Bobolink?" he asked, for sometimes the other was known to play tricks.

"I sure did, Paul, right like this," and stooping over, Bobolink was about to pretend to pick up something when he uttered a gasp.

"Another one!"

He was holding a second coin in his hand, the exact duplicate, so far as they could see, of the first one.

"Must grow here in flocks!" exclaimed Phil; "let's see if we can dig up a whole bunch of 'em, boys!" But although they all started digging with the toes of their shoes, no more shining coins came to light; and it began to look as if Bobolink had been fortunate enough to pick up all there were.

Paul closely examined the two bright quarters.

"If those are queer ones then they'd fool me all right, let me tell you!" declared Bobolink.

"I never saw better in my life," Paul admitted.

The boys were looking pretty serious by now. It began to seem as though that guess made by one of their number could not have been so wide of the mark as at the time some of them believed. Here was pretty strong evidence that these men were engaged in manufacturing spurious coins.

Ought they to consider they had gone far enough, and give up the exploration of the island, returning home to sound the alarm, and send word to the authorities, so that these men might be trapped as they worked?

Paul was tempted to consider that his duty lay that way. Still, there were some things that puzzled him, and made him hesitate before concluding to follow that idea.

Why should they keep the forge out here in the open, when some shelter would seem to be the proper thing, if, as the scouts now believed, they were using the fire to smelt metals, and blend them to the proper consistency for the bad coins?

That was something that puzzled Paul greatly. It caused him to look around in the neighborhood of the forge, in the hope that he might pick up some other clue.

The ground was pretty well trampled over, as though a number of men had been walking back and forth many times in their occupation, whatever it could have been. Paul also saw a number of indentations in the earth, which made him think some heavy object had rested in that open space.

"Whatever they brought here," remarked Jack, presently, "it looks like they must have used some sort of vehicle to carry it; because these tracks have the appearance of ruts made by wheels."

"Rubber tires, too," added Phil. "I've seen too many of 'em not to know; for my father has a garage."

"Is that so?" exclaimed Bobolink, shaking his head, as if to say that with each discovery the mystery, instead of getting lighter, only grew more dense.

"And look how close together they seem to be, would you; a pretty narrow bed for a wagon, don't it seem?" asked Tom Betts.

"But they run off that way," observed Bobolink, "and there are so many of the tracks you can hardly tell which are mates. There's Paul followin' 'em up; reckon we'd better keep with him, boys. We don't want to get separated."

Paul soon came to a stop, and was joined by the others.

"Queer how the marks all seem to knock off about here," he remarked, pointing to the ground. "You can't find one further on. And it isn't that the ground suddenly gets hard, either. This looks the queerest thing of them all. What do they run that thing with wheels up and down here for? Anybody know?"

But silence was the only answer he received, since every one of the six other scouts seemed to be scratching his head, and wrinkling his forehead, as though deep in thought, yet unable to see light.

So they went back to the field forge, to look around again, though their labor was all they had for their pains.

"Not even another lovely quarter to be picked up where it got spilled when they made 'em here, p'raps by the bushel," grumbled Bobolink, scratching the earth with his toe in vain.

He had recovered the coins from Paul, and jingled them in his pocket; though the envious Bluff warned him that they might get him into a peck of trouble, should he be caught by Secret Service men.

"Huh! guess you think you c'n scare me into droppin' them," declared Bobolink, thrusting out his chin at Bluff. "Let me know if you see me doin' it; will you? I c'n just see you falling all over yourself, tryin' to grab these dandy coins, if I let 'em slip by me. Shoot a ball up another alley, Bluff. Go hunt a fortune for yourself, and don't want to grab mine. Hands off, see?"

"Do we go back now, Paul; or had we better keep on to the hill?" Jack asked, as though he knew the other must have been settling this important matter in his mind.

"I think as we've come this far, with the hill just ahead of us, it would be a disappointment not to get up to that cedar tree," Paul replied; at which every one of the other scouts nodded his head.

"W-w-want to s-s-see what the old p-p-place l-l-looks like," remarked Bluff, in his positive way.

"And there's no use in our staying around here any longer, either, I should think," ventured Phil. "How do we know but what some of the men may just happen to butt in on us, while we're looking their old forge over? And if they did, I just guess they'd make things hum for us. So I say, into the woods again for me - the sooner the better."

"I hope we're doing the right thing by keeping on," Paul observed, looking at his companions in a way they took as an invitation to back him up.

"Who's got a better right to go where we feel like?" demanded Bobolink.

"Honest men wouldn't have any kick coming, just because a troop of Boy Scouts happened to camp on their island; and it only goes to show they're doing something shady, that's what. I say go on," Phil gave as his opinion.

Jack, Andy, Bluff and Tom were quick to declare themselves opposed to any change of plan, at least, until after they had reached their goal, which was the foot of the cedar on top of the hill.

This decision seemed to give Paul more heart, and when they left the open space he cast a last glance back at it, as though still puzzled.

The trees grew even more dense as they drew nearer the foot of that peculiar rise in the ground which went to make up what they called a hill. Indeed, the boys were astonished to find such an almost impenetrable jungle.

"Isn't that some sort of shack you can see over yonder?" asked Phil, presently.

As the rest looked, they agreed that it looked like a rude shelter, made out of branches, and some boards fastened together in a crude way.

There was no sign of life about the place, and after making sure of this the scouts grew bold enough to advance upon it from what seemed to be the rear, though this could be settled only by the fact that the entrance to the rustic hut appeared to be on the other side.

Creeping noiselessly up until they were alongside the shelter, the scouts set about finding loopholes through which they might obtain a glimpse of what lay on the other side of those frail walls.

Then one by one they drew back, and the looks they cast at each other indicated that what they had seen was not a pleasant sight.

CHAPTER XXII

THE WIGWAG MESSAGE

The other side of the rough shack was partly open, so that considerable light managed to gain admittance. This had enabled the scouts to see a figure lying on some old blankets, together with the skins of several animals.

It was without doubt the wild man who had given some of their troop such a bad scare when he turned up near the camp soon after their arrival on the island.

He seemed to be sound asleep, and none of them were at all anxious to make any sound calculated to arouse him. Indeed, more than one put a finger to his lips to indicate that they were sealed, as he turned and looked anxiously at his comrades.

Paul made motions to let them know it would be just as well if they quit the vicinity of that queer shack, where the crazy man, as they now deemed him, had his home.

A few minutes later, when they had put enough distance between themselves and the rude shelter to permit conversation, Bobolink could no longer keep his opinions to himself.

"He was a jim-dandy, all right, and a genuine wild man of the woods!" he remarked. "What are the circus fellows thinkin' of, to let such a fine chance slip by to get a real 'What-is-it,' fresh from the jungles of Borneo, half man, and the rest gorilla?"

"And he had Nuthin's dog, after all," observed Paul, quietly.

"What makes you say that, Paul?" asked Jack.

"Because, in the first place, I saw a lot of bones, picked as clean as a whistle, lying on the ground over in a corner. Then there was a lair that looked as if an animal slept in it. And if that wasn't enough, I noticed a piece of broken rope fastened to a stake, close by that corner. You remember I said the dog was dragging a piece of rope around with him, when he came creeping up near our camp last night? He broke away, all right; and I guess the wild man will be minus his dog after this."

"Well, that's one thing settled," asserted Phil "We know now, for sure, there *is* a wild man up here; and some of the officers will have to come and capture him. My father is one of the county freeholders, and he's overseer of the poor in the bargain; so I suppose it'll be up to him to carry out the job. They can't afford to have people say there's a crazy wild man at large, in our district, you see."

"Did any of you notice that there was a rude sort of table in the shack?" asked Paul, as they kept on moving forward, wondering if a third discovery might be made at any minute.

"Well, now, that's a fact," replied Bobolink. "I did see that, but somehow didn't think it queer at the time, not enough to mention it, anyhow. But come to think of it, it was kind of out of the way in the shack of a wild man, eh?"

"There was something on the table that would seem stranger, if you'd noticed it. I saw a battered old coffeepot there!" observed Paul, smiling grimly.

"What?" ejaculated Bobolink. "A wild man liking coffee! Where d'ye suppose he gets the roasted bean? It don't grow on the bushes up here; and he sure don't look as if he had the cash to buy it. Oh! p'raps they use him to pass some of this bogus coin they make! Mebbe he goes to towns, and buys their supplies, all the time they're workin' like beavers up here, makin' the stuff."

"I don't just agree with you there, Bobolink," said Paul. "In the first place, as Phil will tell you, if such a scarecrow ever came into Stanhope, or any other town in the country, the officers would be sure to arrest him, and examine him to see if he oughtn't to be shut up in the asylum. If he got the old pot and the coffee to go with it from these men, then it was in the nature of a bribe not to interfere with their business, as they wanted to stay here on his Island."

"Great brain, Paul; you seem to hit the right idea every time. And chances are, that's just what happened," Bobolink remarked.

"That dog didn't come back," observed Tom Betts.

"And therefore he's still loose," added Phil, uneasily. "Hope we don't run across the beggar again; but if we should, remember Paul, the country expects you to do your duty. You must bag him, no matter what noise you have to make doing it"

"Leave that to me," remarked the scout master. "Now that we know pretty well how the land lies, and whose dog it is, perhaps I won't be so squeamish about shooting the beast if the chance comes along."

"Here's the foot of the rise," Jack broke in.

"And the trees grow more thin as the ground ascends, you notice," Paul went on. He called their attention to all such things, because he was acting as scout master of the troop, and it seemed to him that he should not allow any chance to pass whereby he might enlarge the horizon of scout lore of the lads under him.

"Then it strikes me that we ought to be a bit careful not to show ourselves too plain, as we go up," Jack suggested.

"You're right," added Bobolink. "For all we know, these fellows may have a lookout in a tree, as well as we have, and he'd see us if we got careless. That means we must dodge along, taking advantage of every sort of shelter that crops up. Great fun, boys, and for one I'm just tickled to death over the chance to prove that we learned our little lesson O. K."

All were presently stooping at one moment, where the bushes grew sparse; crawling in among some sheltering rocks at another, and even getting down to wriggle along like so many snakes, when not even so much as a bush offered a means of hiding from observation, in case hostile eyes happened to be turned upwards toward the hilltop at the foot of the lone cedar.

It was not a great distance to cover, and before long they found themselves close to their goal.

Already could they see over the southern side of the island; and after they gained the cedar it would probably be easy to also survey the northern half, the part which doubtless held more of interest to them than any other, since they had reason to believe that the mysterious dwellers on the isle were somewhere there.

"Five more minutes will do it," remarked Paul, when they had gathered in a shallow depression which afforded shelter until they caught their breath again for another climb.

Paul was looking hard at something far beyond the lake. Bobolink, of course, being attracted by his scrutiny, also allowed his gaze to wander in that quarter; but all he saw was what he took to be a buzzard, almost out of sight - a dim speck in the heavens, and about to pass out of sight altogether where clouds hovered above the southern horizon.

"I c'n see about where our camp is," Phil was saying, "and I think I know which tree the signal corps is stationed in. Anyhow, I seem to glimpse something white moving among the green leaves, which, I take it, is a flag being held ready to wave at us."

"I reckon Paul will soon let 'em know we're still on the map," observed Bobolink. "But won't they be s'prised when they learn that we saw the terrible wild man in his own den; and ran across the plant where those rascals make their bogus coin, that looks as bright and good as any Uncle Sam stamps out?"

Just then the leader gave the signal for another advance, and the six scouts who followed set about completing the last leg of the climb.

They finally found themselves at the roots of the cedar tree that crowned the elevation, and which proved of a size far beyond what any of the scouts had imagined.

"Well, here we are at last," said Phil, breathing hard after his exertions.

"And," added Bobolink, also badly winded, though he would chatter; "now to see Paul get one of the other fellows on the line, to wig his wag at us, or do something that sounds that way. There he goes at it. And looky there, they've been watching us climb, I reckon, because almost before Paul made the first sign, that other fellow began sendin'."

They watched the fluttering red flag with the white centre. Some of them had taken more or less interest in sending and receiving messages; but the boy in the tree proved too fast for any of them to follow. They suspected that it was Jud Elderkin himself; for outside of Paul and Jack, he was the best hand at that sort of thing.

"My stars! he keeps right along doing it; don't he?" muttered Bobolink.

"Must be some message, too, believe me," added Phil.

"N-n-now, what d'ye s-s-suppose has happened at c-c-camp since we q-q-quit?" remarked Bluff, anxiously waiting for the message to be translated.

Not once did Paul break in on the sending of the message. He sat there, close to the base of the big cedar which sheltered his back from the north side of the island; and seemed to be wholly engrossed in transcribing the various signs of the flag code.

They could not see the boy in the branches of the tree; but from their elevated position the white and red flag was in plain view. Up and down, and crosswise, it continued to write its message, that was doubtless like printed letters to Paul and Jack, while unintelligible to those who had never taken lessons in wigwagging.

Finally came the well known sign that the message was done; and that the sender awaited the wishes of the party with whom he was in communication.

Paul turned upon his comrades. They saw that the frown had come back again to his usually smooth forehead, as though he had learned something to add to the perplexities of the problem they were trying so diligently to solve.

"It's Jud," he said, simply, "and he's just sent an astonishing message. This is the way it ran, boys: 'Presence here known. Man in aeroplane passed over camp. Went down lake half hour ago. Out of sight now. Answer!'"

No wonder Bobolink fairly held his breath, and the other five scouts looked at each other, as though they could hardly believe their ears. For a full minute they sat there and stared; while Bobolink remembered the far-away black object that, at the time, he had thought to be a buzzard.

CHAPTER XXIII

STILL FLOUNDERING IN THE MIRE

"Whee!"

It was, of course, Bobolink who gave utterance to this characteristic exclamation.

Like most of the others, he had been so stunned by the message read by Paul, that for the moment he failed to find words to express his feelings.

An aeroplane had passed over the camp! And heading south, which would take it toward the quarter where Stanhope lay!

Here they had thought themselves so far removed from civilization that the only persons within a range of miles might be set down as a wild man and some lawless counterfeiters, who had chosen this region because of its inaccessibility.

And now they had learned that one of the latest inventions of the day had been moving above the island, with the pilot actually looking down on the camp, and so discovering the fact of the Boy Scouts having returned after their banishment from the place.

No wonder they all stared at each other, and that speech was denied them for a time.

Jack was the first to speak. He had read the message, being nearly as good a signalman as Paul or Jud.

"Things seem to be picking up at a pretty lively clip for us; eh, fellows?" was the way he put it.

"Picking up?" gasped Bobolink; "Seems to me they're getting to the red hot stage about as fast as they can. An aeroplane! And up here on our desert island at that, which folks said was given over to spooks and wild men! That *is* the limit, sure! Hold me, somebody; I think I'm going to faint!"

But as nobody made any movement in that direction, Bobolink changed his mind.

"Let's look into this thing a little closer, fellows," said Paul, always prompt to set an investigation going.

"That's what!" echoed Bluff, surprising himself by not stammering a particle, even though he was still quivering with excitement.

"Jud says an aeroplane passed over the camp; but he didn't tell whether it rose from the island or not, though the chances are that it did," Paul continued.

"Why do you say that as if you felt sure?" demanded Tom Betts.

"Yes," put in Phil, eagerly, "you've got on to something, Paul; give us a chance to grab it, too, please."

"Sure I will," complied the scout master, cheerfully. "And I'm only surprised that one of you, always so quick to see such things, hasn't jumped on to this little game as soon as I have. Look back a short time, and you'll remember how we were scratching our heads over the tracks of wheels down in that big opening!"

"Wheels!" exclaimed Bobolink, with fresh excitement. "Well, I should say yes; and looks to me like we had 'em in our heads too, where the brains ought to be. Wheels, yes, and rubber-tired wheels too! Remember how they seemed to run up and down a regular track, and just went so far, when they gave out? Whoop! why, it's as easy as two and two make four. Anybody ought to have guessed that."

"Huh!" remarked Tom Betts, scornfully; "that's what they said, you recollect, when Columbus discovered America. After you know, everything looks easy. In my mind Paul goes up head. He's in a class by himself."

"And that forge might have been used, among other things, for doing all sorts of mending metal pieces connected with an aeroplane," Paul went on, smiling at Tom's tribute of praise.

"Not forgetting these sort of things," Bobolink observed, positively, as he took out a pair of bright new quarters, and jingled them musically in his hand.

"Well, we haven't had any reason to change our minds about that thing, - yet," said Paul. "But what strikes me as the queerest of all is the fact that while we must have been pretty close by when that aeroplane went up, how was it none of us heard the throbbing of the engine?"

They looked at each other in bewilderment. Paul's query had opened up a vast field of conjecture. One and all shook their heads.

"I pass," declared Tom.

"Me too," added Phil.

"Must 'a got some new kind of motor aboard that is silent," suggested Jack.

"J-j-just a-goin' to s-s-say that, when Jack t-t-took the

w-w-words out of m-m-my m-m-mouth," Bluff exploded.

"No trouble doin' that, Bluff," laughed Bobolink. "If that aeroplane did climb up out of that field, while we pushed through the heavy timber, and none of us heard a thing, let me tell you, boys, they've got a cracker-jack of a motor, that's what!"

"But arrah! would ye be thinkin' that a lot of bog-trottin' counterfeiters'd be havin' a rale aeroplane?" burst out Andy Flinn, who had up to now been unable to give any expression to his feelings.

"I'd say these fellers must be a pretty tony lot, that's all," Bobolink declared.

"Whatever do you suppose they use such a machine for?" asked Tom.

Again all eyes were turned upon Paul, as the oracle of the group of wondering scouts. He shrugged his shoulders, as if he thought he had as much right as any of the others to admit that he was puzzled.

"Well, we'd have to make a stab at guessing that," he observed. "Any one thing of half a dozen might be the truth. An aeroplane could be used for carrying the stuff they make up here to a distant market. Then again, it might be only a sort of plaything, or hobby, of the chief money-maker; something he amuses himself with, to take his mind off business. All men have hobbies - fishing, hunting, horse racing, golf - why couldn't this chap take to flying for his fun?"

"That sounds good to me," declared Bobolink; "anyhow, we know he must be a kind of high-flier."

"Seems like our mystery bulges bigger than ever," remarked Phil, frowning.

"It does, for a fact," admitted Tom; "instead of finding out things, we're getting deeper in the mud all the time."

"Oh! I don't know," Paul said, musingly; and although the rest instantly turned upon him, fully expecting that the scout master would have some sort of communication to make, he did not think it worth while, at that time, to explain what he meant.

"Say, I wonder, now, if we could see anything of those fellows from up here?" remarked Bobolink, suddenly.

"That's so," echoed Phil, perceiving what the other intended to convey; "we can see the whole of the island now; and if they're camped somewhere on the north end, perhaps we might get a glimpse of canvas."

"What makes you think these men have their headquarters on the north end, rather than anywhere else?" asked Paul, quickly.

"Why, when we got up here, I noticed that smoke was climbing up over there; and smoke means a fire; which also tells that some person must be around to look after it," replied Phil, promptly.

"Pretty good reasoning," said Paul, nodding his head toward Phil; for if anything gave him pleasure as scout master of the troop, it was to see a boy using his head.

All now looked over the crown of the hill, toward the upper end of the island. The first thing they saw, of course, was the thin column of smoke which Phil had mentioned. Then Bobolink burst out with:

"And you were right, Paul, when you said that the chances were the island was close to the north side of the lake, so animals could swim across. Why, only a narrow streak of water separates 'em there, sure enough."

"Oh! that was only a guess on my part," Paul confessed. "I saw about how far away the mainland trended up there, and supposed that our island must run near it in places. I'm pleased to see that I hit the mark, for once at least, in this mixed-up mess."

Paul was evidently more or less provoked because he had been unable to understand many of the strange things that had happened since their arrival on Cedar Island. And the others knew that he was taking himself to task because of his dullness; but what of them, if the scout master needed to be wakened up - where did they come in?

"I can't be sure about it," observed Phil, who had been looking intently at one particular spot; "but it seems as if I could make out the roof of a shed of some kind, over yonder, close to where the smoke rises."

This set them all to looking again. Andy, who had very good eyes, declared he could make it out, and that it was a roof of some kind; one or two of the others, after their attention had been called to the spot, also admitted that it did look a little that way, though they could not say for a certainty.

"Anyhow, I reckon that's where these men live," Paul declared; "and now the question is, are we going to turn back here; or keep right on exploring this queer old Cedar Island?"

Bobolink, who was busy cutting his initials in the bark of the big cedar that topped the squatty hill, spoke first of all; for being an impetuous fellow, he seldom thought twice before airing his opinions.

"Me to push right on," he said. "What difference does it make to us that some other fellows chance to be camping on the same island? It's free to all. We aren't going to bother them one whit, if only they leave us alone. But they began wrong, you see, when they told us to get off the earth. That riled me. I never did like to be sat on by anybody. It just seems like something inside gets to workin' overtime, and all my badness begins to rise up, like mom's yeast in a batch of dough. Count my vote to go on ahead, Paul."

"Well, who's next?" asked the scout master "and remember, that when it comes to a matter like this, I always try and do what the majority wants."

"I'm willing to do what the rest say," came from Jack.

"Go right on, and make a clean job of it," said Tom Betts, grimly.

"S-s-same here!" jerked out Bluff.

"That spakes my mind to a dot, so it do," Andy followed.

Paul threw up his hand.

"Enough said; that makes four in favor already, and settles the matter. I won't tell you which way I would have voted, because the thing's been taken from my hands. And besides, I would only have considered your welfare in making my decision, and not my own desire."

"Which manes he would have said yis for himsilf, and no for the rist of us," declared the Irish boy, exultantly; "so it's glad I am we've made up our minds to go on. Whin do we shtart, Paul, darlint?"

"Right away," replied the one addressed. "There's no use staying any longer up here, unless you think I'd better get Jud again, and wigwag him all that we've learned up to now."

"It'll keep," said Phil, hastily, for he wanted to see the faces of those other scouts when the several astonishing pieces of news were told; especially about the finding of the real wild man asleep, the discovery of the field forge in the open glade and the picking up of the two silver quarters, which last he felt sure would give them all a surprise.

"A11 right!" the scout master announced, "I think pretty much the same way; and besides, it would take a long while sending all that news. But perhaps I ought to let the boys know we're going on further; and that they needn't expect us much before the middle of the afternoon. That'll give us plenty of time to roam around, and perhaps come back another way."

So he started once more to catch the attention of Jud, perched high up in that tree above the sink near the lower end of the island, where he could have an uninterrupted view of the cedar on the top of the hill.

Then there was a fluttering of the signal flag and briefly the scout master informed the other as to what their intentions were.

"That job's done," Paul remarked, presently, when Jud replied with a gesture that implied his understanding the message; "and now to move down-hill again. We're taking some big chances in what we're expecting to do, fellows, and I only hope it won't prove a mistake. Come along!"

CHAPTER XXIV

THE DISCOVERY

"There's one thing that I think we haven't bothered our heads much about, Paul," remarked Jack, just before they quitted the vicinity of the big cedar on top of the hill.

"What?" asked Bobolink, cocking his head on one side to see how well his initials looked in the bark of the tree from which Cedar Island took its name; and which would tell later explorers that others had been there ahead of them.

"Why, it seems to me those clouds down there on the southern horizon have a look that spells storm," Jack continued.

"Wow! wonder if we will strike another rainy spell?" said Bobolink, so quickly that none of the others had a chance to get a word in; "that last one helped us get out of the mud in the canal; if another comes will it be as accommodatin', or turn on us, and whoop things up, carrying our tents away over the island, and losing 'em in the swamps beyond there?"

"Oh! say, don't imagine so much, Bobolink," interrupted Phil. "You're the greatest fellow I ever saw for figuring all sorts of bad things out long before they ever get a chance to start. What Jack means is, will we be apt to get caught in the rain, and be soaked?"

"That's the main thing," added Tom Betts, who was rather

particular about how his khaki suit looked on him, for Tom was a bit of a "dresser," as some of the others, less careful with regard to their looks, called it.

"I've noticed that it's grown pretty close and muggy," Paul went on.

"I should say it had," added Bobolink. "I kept moppin' my face most of the way up the rise. Thought we'd sure get a fine breeze after reachin' the top; but nixey, nothing doing. It's as dead as a door nail; or Julius Caesar ever was. Yes, that spells rain before night, I'd like to risk my reputation as a weather prophet in saying."

"Still, we go on?" Paul asked.

"Well, we'd be a fine lot of scouts," blurted out Bobolink, "if the chance of getting our backs wet made us give up a plan we'd decided on."

"Lead the way, Paul; they're bent on finding out something more about these men. And feeling that way, as Bobolink says, a little rain storm wouldn't make them change their minds," and Jack, while speaking, started after the scout master, who had commenced to descend the hill.

They did not immediately turn toward the north side. There seemed no use in deliberately making their presence known to any one stationed over at the north end of the island, providing the mysterious men were not already aware of it.

Paul, when doing his wigwag act, had been careful to keep the crest of the hill between his flag and that suspicious quarter where the smoke column was lazily creeping up, as smoke has a habit of doing just before rain comes.

Of course it might be possible that the man in the aeroplane, after discovering the tents in the sink, may have made some sort of signal that would tell his comrades the fact of the scouts having returned in the night.

Paul wished, now that it was too late, he had thought to ask Jud about that point. It might be of some benefit to them to know whether the men were aware of their presence; or rested serene in the belief that they were the only occupants of the island, besides the wild man.

After the scouts had gone down a little way, Paul began to change his course. He was now turning toward the north. The trees grew much more thickly here, and would surely screen them from observation.

The boys had resumed their former habit of observing everything that came in their way, as true scouts always should. They turned their heads from right to left and Bobolink even looked back of him more than a few times. Perhaps he remembered that there was a wild man at large who might take a notion to awake from his sleep, and, discovering the scout patrol, think it his business to follow them.

And then, to be sure, they ought to keep in mind the fact concerning that wild dog that had gone back to the habits of its ancestors, preferring to live by hunting, rather than take food from the hand of man. It would be far from pleasant to have old Lion suddenly sneak up on them, and give them a scare.

But everything seemed peaceful around them. Now and then a bird would fly out of a thicket, or give a little burst of song from the branch of some tree. A red-headed woodpecker tapped boisterously on the dead top of a beech near by, trying hard to arouse the curiosity of the worms that lived there, so as to cause them to poke out their heads to see who was so noisy at their front doors; when of course the feathered hammerer stood ready to gobble them up.

"Oh!" gasped Bobolink, when there was a sudden whirring sound of wings, and they had a furtive glimpse of something flashing through the undergrowth near by.

"It's only a partridge; don't be worried!" remarked Phil.

"Sure it was," muttered Bobolink, with scorn; "any fellow with only one eye'd know that *now*; but all the same, the thing gave me a bad turn, I'm that keyed up."

"And that's a cotton-tail looking at us over yonder, so don't throw another fit when he takes a notion to skip out," Phil continued, pointing with his cudgel to where a rabbit sat, observing the intruders, as though wondering what business any human beings had coming to the island that had been left alone so long.

Presently the little animal skipped off a few paces and then stopped again. As the scouts advanced, it repeated these tactics; indeed, so tame did it seem that any of them could have easily hit the rabbit with a stone, had they felt so inclined, which, as scouts, they could not think of doing.

"Looks like she's got a litter of young ones close by here," said Bobolink; "and is playing lame just to lead us away from the bunch. I've seen rabbits do that before now. The cuteness of the thing! Look at her, would you, just beggin' us to run after, and try to capture her?"

"I've seen a partridge act as if she had a broken wing," Jack remarked, quietly; "and flutter along the ground in a way that couldn't help but make one try to catch her; but if you chased after her, it would be to see the old bird take wing pretty soon, and go off like a rocket."

"Same here," declared Paul; "and going back, I flushed a whole covey of the prettiest little birds you ever saw. They'd been crouching under a bush while the old one played lame; just as if she'd told them all about it. But I heard her calling in the brush later on, and of course she got them all together again."

"There goes your lame rabbit now, Bobolink; and say, look at the way she jumps over the ground," remarked Phil, chuckling.

"Not so loud, boys," cautioned the scout master. "These things are all mighty interesting; but we mustn't forget what we're here for nor yet the fact that we've got a pretty good hunch there are some men close by who would be just as mad as hops if they knew we meant to stalk their camp and spy on them. If you have to say anything, whisper it softly, remember."

At that they all fell silent. It was true that they had forgotten for the moment that they were doing scouting work; and under such conditions talking was not allowed, especially above the lowest tone.

All of them noticed that it was getting very close now, for they had to use the red bandanna handkerchiefs they carried, and quite frequently at that, to wipe away the perspiration that oozed from their foreheads.

"Lucky we left our coats in camp; isn't it?" remarked Phil.

"Looks that way now, but if that rain does strike us, we may wish we had 'em on," Tom Betts replied; showing that he at least had not been able to put out of his head the possibility of a storm.

"Seems to me we must be getting somewhere," Phil observed.

"It can't be very much further," Paul answered, feeling that the remark was addressed to him as the pilot of the expedition."

"I should say not," came from Bluff, as chipper as a bird's song, and without the least sign of halt or break; "if we go on much more, we'll walk off the end of the island."

Bobolink patted him on the back, as if to encourage him in well doing.

"That's the stuff, Bluff; you c'n do it when you try," he whispered; "but as to steppin' into the lake, I guess we aren't that near the north end yet, by a good sight."

Paul nodded his head, but said nothing; from that Bobolink knew the scout master agreed with him. They could go considerably longer without being halted by coming to the water's edge.

Jack called the attention of his chums just then to something ahead.

"Seems to me I smell smoke," he said, "and if you bend down here, so you can look under the branches of the trees, you'll see something that's got the shape of a shed, or cabin, off yonder."

The others, upon making a try, agreed with Jack that it did seem that way.

"Oh! we're right on top of the nest, all right" chattered Bobolink, but showing his wisdom by keeping his voice down to its lowest note; "and now, if we c'n duplicate that little dodge we played at the shack of the wild man, it's goin' to be as easy as turning over off a spring-board, with a ten foot drop."

"But if we're caught we might get shot at," suggested Phil, as if the idea had struck him for the first time that they were really playing with fire, in thus bearding desperate lawbreakers in their den.

"We aren't going to get caught," said Bobolink; "who's afraid? Not I. Lead along, Paul. I want to get this thing out of my system, so I c'n have a little rest up here," and he placed a hand on his brow.

Although himself doubtful as to the wisdom of the move, Paul could not back down now, after allowing the boys to vote on the matter. Perhaps he was more or less sorry that at the time he had not exercised his privilege as scout master to put his foot down on their taking any more chances, just to satisfy such curiosity as reckless fellows like Bobolink might feel, with regard to the unknown men.

It was too late now. Until some of the boys themselves manifested a desire to call the retreat, he must go on; although it began to seem more than ever audacious - this creeping up on a den of men who were hiding from the eye of the law in order to carry on their nefarious trade.

And so they started to creep forward, now dodging behind trees, and crawling back of friendly patches of bushes whenever the chance presented itself. It was all exciting enough, to be sure, and doubtless gave the boys many a delightful little thrill.

In this fashion they came upon a larger clump of trees and bushes, which, instead of trying to round, they concluded to pass through.

It was just as they gained a point inside this clump that they were brought up with a round turn by discovering a couple of objects standing there, as though they had been left behind when the valuable contents which they formerly encased had been taken out.

These were two large packing cases, of unusual shape, and made of heavy planed boards!

Some of the scouts looked at them carelessly, for to them these objects did not carry any particular meaning. Not so Jack, Tom Betts and Bobolink. Those three boys had received a shock, as severe as it was unexpected.

They recognized those cases as being the identical ones which had only lately reposed snugly in the planing mill of Jack's father in Stanhope, and to guard which one Hans Waggoner had been hired by the man who owned them, Professor Hackett! And as they stood there and gaped, doubtless among the many things that flashed into the minds of those three lads was the fact that *somebody* had been trying to get to see what the contents of those mysterious cases might be; which person they now knew must have been a Government Secret Service man, a detective from Washington, on the track of the bold counterfeiting gang!

All these things, and much more, flashed through the minds of Jack and his chums, as they stood there in that thicket, and stared hard at the two big cases bound around with twisted wire, but which had now been relieved of their unknown contents, for they stood empty.

And the others, realizing that something had occurred out of the regular channel, waited for them to speak, and explain what they had discovered.

CHAPTER XXV

TIME TO GO BACK

"What is it, Bobolink - Jack?" asked the scout master.

"The boxes yonder!" Bobolink managed to exclaim.

"You evidently have seen them before; tell me, Jack, are they the ones you said your father stored for that man?" continued Paul.

"They certainly look mighty like them," replied the other; "and you know, they were taken away that morning early. They must have been carried across country to the shore of the lake, and then ferried over in a rowboat. That was what we saw the marks of, and the four men walked off with these between them."

"Whee! did you ever?" gasped the still bewildered Bobolink. "Yes, here you c'n see the markin' on the lid they threw away when they opened this one - 'Professor Hackett, In care of John Stormways, Stanhope,' all as plain as anything. And to think how after all my worryin' the old boxes have bobbed up here. Don't it beat the Dutch how things turn out?"

That seemed to be the one thing that gripped Bobolink's attention - the strange way in which those two heavy boxes with the twisted wire binding had happened to cross his path again.

But Paul was thinking of other things, that might have a more serious bearing on the case. He turned to Jack again.

"What do you know about this so-called professor?" he asked.

"Me? Why, next to nothing, only that he comes from down near New York City at a place called Coney Island, where lots of fakirs hold out; and plenty of men too, in the summer season, who would want to circulate a little money that did not bear the Government stamp."

"But your father seems to have known him; or at any rate believed he was a law-abiding citizen," pursued Paul; "otherwise he would hardly have given him the privilege of storing his cases in his mill over night."

"Oh! my father is that easy-going, nearly anybody could pull the wool over his eyes. He believed the yarn this pretended professor told him, I've no doubt, and thought it next door to nothing to let him keep the boxes in the mill for a short time. You know, my father is the best-hearted man in Stanhope, barring none. But I agree with the rest of you that this time he must have got stung. The professor is sure a bad egg. I must put my dad wise as soon as I get half a chance."

"Perhaps it's already too late to save him from getting stuck with a lot of the stuff they manufacture?" suggested Tom Betts.

"Oh! that could hardly be so," Jack replied, cheerfully. "When these bogus money-makers want to get rid of some of their stock they always have go-betweens do the job for them. It would be too easy tracing things if they passed the stuff themselves. So I guess my dad hasn't taken in any great amount of the counterfeits."

Bobolink was down on his knees. He even crawled into one of the overturned boxes, as though trying hard to ascertain from sundry marks what could have been contained under that wooden cover.

He came out, shaking his head, as though his efforts had not been attended by success.

"Looks like machinery of some kind, that's all I c'n tell," he admitted. "But of course, they'd need a press of some sort to work off the paper money on. Now, chances are, it's bein' put up right in that long shed yonder, that we c'n see. Question is, how're we goin' to get close enough to peek through a crack, and find out what's goin' on in there?"

Again did most of the boys look uneasily at each other. Paul believed that, now the great test had arrived, they were beginning to weaken a little. No doubt it did not seem so glorious a thing when you got close up, this spying on a band of lawless men, who would be apt to deal harshly with eavesdroppers, if caught in the act.

Still, he would not give the order to retreat unless they asked for it. They had been allowed to settle that matter when they voted; it was up to Bobolink, Tom, Bluff or Andy to start the ball rolling, if they began to reconsider their hasty conclusion of a while back.

Bobolink looked toward the low, long shed, now plainly seen, in something of a rocky opening, with glimpses of water beyond which told how close to the shore it had been built. But he did not act as though as anxious to rush matters as before.

"Why d'ye believe they ever landed those boxes where they did, and toted 'em all the way up here, heavy as they were, when there's the water close by?" asked Jack.

"I was thinking about that a minute ago," replied Paul; "and the only explanation I can find is this: Perhaps the water is mighty shallow all around up at the north end of the island. I can see that the shore is rocky, and if that's so, then no boat with a heavy load could get close enough in to land the stuff. And so they had to get busy, and carry the boxes, one at a time."

"Sounds reasonable, and we'll let her go at that," commented Bobolink, who, as a rule, was contented to take Paul's opinion.

Paul himself stooped down to take a look into the cases. He did not make any remark as he straightened up again, nor did any of the others think to ask his opinion; which possibly may have been lucky, for perhaps Paul would not have liked to commit himself just then. If he had found anything that gave him a new clue, he was evidently keeping it to himself until he could get more proof.

"S'pose we ought to make a fresh start," suggested Bobolink, but with a lack of eagerness that was plainly noticeable; it was as though the discovery of those two mysterious boxes under such strange conditions had rather cooled his ardor.

"That's so," remarked Tom.

"We've g-g-got so n-n-near now, we ought to f-f-finish!" Bluff declared.

And yet none of them made the slightest movement looking to an advance, a fact that Paul could not help but notice, and which warned him they were close to the point of a change of policy. A suggestion that they give up the spy business at this stage, and retreat in good order to their camp, would doubtless have met with favor, and been sure of a unanimous vote.

But still Paul, having his own notions of such matters, when dealing with boys, declined to say anything. If one of the four who were mainly responsible for their being there should take it upon himself to offer such a motion, he would only too gladly put it to a vote. Until such time came he must continue to remain silent.

"Just as you say, boys; I'm carrying out your plans," he remarked, quietly, wishing to let them know that they had it in their own power to alter conditions at any time they so desired.

They all finally moved after the scout master, even if some feet did lag a little. Bluff and Phil particularly were conscious of a strange sinking sensation in the region of their hearts, which they mistrusted signified fear; and rather than have any of their comrades suspect that they had a cold hand pressing there, they shut their teeth hard together, and determined that under no circumstances would they show the white feather.

So Paul led them on.

Again they tried to conceal themselves as best they might in devious ways. Here the wide and generous trunk of a friendly tree afforded them a certain amount of shelter; a little further on a small pile of rocks answered the same benevolent purpose; but always the main idea was to hide from any curious eyes that might be on the lookout in the vicinity of that queer looking shed - newly made, if the fresh boards signified anything.

"Looky here! there's a man!" suddenly exclaimed Bobolink.

The others had discovered the man at about the same time. They all lay flat and hardly dared breathe, lest in some manner they attract the attention of the stranger, who seemed to be not only a big man, but rather a fierce-looking fellow in the bargain.

He was glancing all around at the heavens, as though wondering whether the aeroplane was not coming back, whatever its mission in flying away south could have been. Standing there, he shaded his eyes with his hands and continued to look toward the south for several minutes. Then he made a gesture as of disappointment, and vanished around the corner of the shed.

"Never looked down this way once!" Bobolink said triumphantly, as though their escape had caused his spirits to rise a little.

"That leaves the coast clear again, anyhow," said Tom Betts, as if he now had a rather disagreeable duty to perform, which, since it had to be done, had better be gotten through with as speedily as possible.

When leaving camp these brave scouts had never dreamed but that spying upon the enemy would prove the most delightful task imaginable. Even later on, when they had voted to keep moving forward, with so much assurance, the picture had not begun to fade; but now it did not seem the same.

As the shelter grew less and less, however, it became evident that presently, if they continued to advance in this fashion, they must reach a point where, in order to make progress, they must expose themselves to hostile eyes, should any be on the watch.

Would even this cause one of the four scouts to "take water," as Bobolink called it, and make the sign that he had had enough?

Paul knew them all pretty well, and he also realized the fact that every fellow possessed a nature bordering on the stubborn. It was the dread of being thought cowardly that kept them from taking the cue from Paul, and ending this foolish advance.

They had gone over fifty feet since the last stop, and passed the last large tree which could be looked on to give them any shelter.

It was just at this moment that once again the big man was seen coming hastily around the corner of the shed.

At sight of him the boys stood still. There was no use trying to hide now. Perhaps some faint hope took possession of them that they might be unnoticed if they did not move; just as the still hunter, stalking a feeding deer, will watch its short tail, and whenever he sees it twitch he stands perfectly motionless; for he knows that the animal is about to raise his head, and that he will probably be taken for a stump if he does not move hand or foot.

But evidently the man had sighted the seven khaki-clad scouts. He seemed almost petrified with amazement at first, and stood staring at them. As if awaking from his trance, he began to make frantic motions with his arms, and at the same time shouted hoarsely at them:

"Go back! Get out of that! You're crazy staying there! Run, I tell you, while you have the chance! Get away! Get away, you fools!"

The scouts looked at each other in astonishment. What could it all mean? Were all the men on this queer island stark, staring crazy? He called them that, but it is always a rule for mad people to believe every one else crazy but themselves.

"Say, what does the guy mean?" cried Bobolink, who seemed to be utterly unable to understand a thing; "mebbe it's a small-pox hospital we've run on, fellows!"

But Paul was beginning to see a light. Possibly the excited gestures, as well as the urgent words of the big man, may have assisted him to arrive at a conclusion.

He no longer felt so decided about not speaking the word that would cause his little detachment to turn and retreat. There must be danger hovering over them, danger in some terrible form, to make that unknown man so urgent.

"Let's get out of this, boys!" he called, "every fellow turn, and streak it as fast as he can. And get behind trees as quick as you can, because -"

They had already started to obey the scout master, and possibly had covered a few jumps when it seemed that the very earth shook and quivered under them, as a fearful roar almost deafened every boy.

Just as you have seen a pack of cards, made into tent shape in a curving row, go falling down when the first one is touched, so those seven scouts were knocked flat by some concussion of the air.

They had hardly fallen than one and all scrambled to their feet, and fled madly from the scene, as if fearful lest the whole end of the island might be blown up behind them, and catch them in a trap from which there could be no escape.

CHAPTER XXVI

HONORABLE SCARS

So it turned out after all that the scout master did not have to change his mind, and give the order for retreat. When that dreadful panic overwhelmed the scouts, it was really a case of "every one for himself."

Either by rare good luck, or some sort of instinct, the seven lads managed to keep pretty well together as they ran. Not a single fellow dreamed of allowing himself to get separated from his comrades. It seemed to be a case of "united we stand, divided we fall," or "in union there is strength."

If in their mad rush some of the boys collided with trees, or stumbled over obstacles that they failed to discover in time, they were not of a mind to let such trifles interfere with their making record time.

In such cases it was only necessary to scramble erect again, and put on a little extra spurt in order to overhaul their comrades.

What had taken them half an hour to cover when they were "scouting" in such approved fashion, was passed over in about five minutes.

It was Paul who came to his senses first. He realized that there was no one chasing them and that, to tell the truth, not one of the boys could have been seriously hurt by what had befallen.

George A. Warren

So he began to laugh, and the sound reaching the ears of the others, appeared to act on their excited minds like soothing balm.

Gradually the whole lot slackened their pace until they were going at a jog trot; which in turn settled down to a walk.

Finally Bobolink came to a full stop.

"Whee! let's get a few decent breaths, fellows!" he managed to gasp.

The others were apparently nothing loth, and so they all drew up in a bunch. A sorry lot they looked just then, to tell the truth. It seemed as though nearly every fellow had some distinguishing mark.

Phil's rather aristocratic face had a long scratch that extended down the right side, and gave him a queer look; Jack was caressing a lump on his forehead, which he may have received from a tree, or else when he was knocked down without warning by that singular explosion; Andy was trying to quench a nose-bleed, and needed his face washed the worst way; Bluff's left eye seemed partly closed, as if he had been too close to the business end of an angry bee; while Bobolink had two or three small cuts about his face that made him look as if he had been trying to tattoo himself - with wretched success.

So they looked at one another, and each thought the balance of the crowd had the appearance of a set of lunatics on the rampage.

Hardly had they stared at each other than they set to laughing.

"Oh! my stars! but aren't you a screamer though, Andy, with all that blood smeared over your face; and Bluff, why he looks as if he'd been in a prize fight!" was the way Bobolink expressed his feelings, bending over as he laughed.

"Huh! you're not so very pretty yourself!" replied Bluff, with not the slightest sign of an impediment in his speech - evidently it had been frightened out of his system for the time being. "Anybody'd think you were a South Sea Islander on the warpath. And wouldn't they cross over to the other side of the road in a hurry if they met you! Say, if Mazie Kenwood or Laura Carson could only see you now, they'd give you the cut straight."

"Look at Jack's bump, would you?" Tom Betts exclaimed.

"Don't call attention to me any more than you can help," Jack remarked, making a wry face, as he caressed the protuberance on his forehead; "it feels as big as a walnut, let me tell you, and hurts like fun. The sooner I'm back in camp, so I can slap some witch hazel on that lump, the better it'll please me, boys."

After a little more laughing and grumbling, Paul, who had escaped without any visible hurts, though he walked a little lame, remarked:

"Well, do we start right back again, and take a look-in on those men? Don't everybody speak at once, now!"

All the same they did, and the burden of the united protest was that circumstances alter cases; that they had arrived at the conclusion that what those men were doing on the island could be no affair of honest, law-abiding scouts; and that as for them, the camp in the sink offered more attractions at that particular moment than anything else they could think of.

Of course that settled it. The scouting was over for that occasion. They had done themselves credit, as far as it went; but then, who would ever dream that they would come within an ace of being blown sky-high with the whole upper end of the island?

As if by common consent, they started to move forward again, and every fellow seemed to know, as if by instinct, which was south, and whereabouts the camp was, for they needed no pilot now.

And as they journeyed they talked it all over. Every boy seemed to have an opinion of his own with regard to what had happened, and they differed radically.

"Tell you what," said Tom Betts, who had also escaped with only a few minor injuries, because he was as quick as a cat, and must have fallen on a soft piece of ground besides; "tell you what, I thought that old hill had turned into a volcano, and just bust all to flinders."

"Well, now," Phil admitted, "I somehow had an idea that storm had chased up when we didn't chance to be watching, and lightning had struck a tree close to the place where we happened to be standing looking at that crazy man wave his arms."

"Me?" Bobolink remarked; "why, I was dead sure what we guessed about a war game bein' played up here between two pretended hostile armies was right; and that one of 'em had blown up the fort of the other. You see, that aeroplane had a sorter military air about it, even if I didn't see it. And I'm not sure yet it isn't that."

"One thing sure," remarked Paul; "the man was trying to warn us to keep back, for he knew some sort of mine was going to explode, and that we might be killed. As it was, we got off pretty lucky, I think. This sprain will heal in a day or two; but if a rock weighing a ton or two had dropped down on me, I guess the chances of my ever seeing Stanhope again would have been mighty slim."

"But tell me," Bobolink asked, "what in the world would counterfeiters want with exploding mines, and doin' all that sort of thing? Just remember that big bang we had the other night, that woke everybody up. Shows it's a habit with 'em, and that this wasn't some freak accident. Gee! my head's buzzing around so I can't think straight. Somebody do my guessin' for me; won't you, please?"

"That's right," said Tom Betts, suddenly; "who are these men, anyway? P'raps we didn't size 'em up straight when we made up our minds they were bogus money-makers. Mebbe they happen to be a different sort of crowd altogether. How about that, Paul; am I off my trolley when I say that?"

"I've been beginning to believe something was crooked in our guess for a little while, Tom," replied the scout master; "but all the same, you've got me up in the air when you ask who and what they are. I'm rattled more than I've been in many a day, to be honest with you all."

Bobolink took out something from his pocket. He stared hard at the two shining quarters, and jingled them in his hand.

"Look good to me," he was heard to say; "I'd pass 'em any time for genuine. But what silly chump'd be throwing good money around like that, tell me?"

"Or bad money either, Bobolink," remarked Paul; "so you see, it was an accident in any case. You've lost money many a time out of your pocket; well, this man was in the same boat. Chances are, that's straight goods."

Bobolink grinned.

"If that's so," he remarked calmly, "I'm in a half dollar, and that's some satisfaction. But say, what a time we'll have tellin' the boys. Wow! I can see the eyes of Little Billie, and Curly, and Nuthin just stickin' out of their heads when they hear all we've run up against."

"And we'd better move along a little faster while about it," observed Paul.

"Why? Hope you don't think any of those men are chasin' after us; or that we'll run up against that wild man, or the big yellow dog again?" Bobolink inquired, glancing fearfully about him.

"No, I was considering the feelings of the boys," replied the scout master.

"That's a fact," Jack went on, "they'll be worried about us, after hearing that terrible report, and think something has happened to our crowd. But we're not a great way from camp now, Paul."

"No, and if the distance was greater, I'd stop long enough to send up a smoke signal that would tell Jud we were all right. But that'd take time, and perhaps we'd better hurry along," and the scout master set a new pace, even though limping slightly.

"Got hurt some yourself; did you, Paul?" Jack asked, solicitously.

"Oh! only a little sprain, but it happens to be on a muscle that I have to use when I walk, and you know a fellow favors such a pain. But I can see where the sink lies now; we'll be there in ten minutes, perhaps half that."

They continued to push on. For the time being most of them forgot about their personal troubles, in their anxiety to join their comrades. And Bobolink, as he walked beside Jack, spoke what was on his mind:

"It was a grand old scare, all right, and one we won't ever forget, believe me; but there's one thing that tickles me half to death, Jack. We know *now* where the queer old boxes went to, even if we are up in the air about what was in them. And the chances are we may find that out before we're done with this business; because those men ought to come down and ask if anybody got hurt by their silly Fourth of July fireworks display. There's the camp, boys. Whoopee!"

CHAPTER XXVII

ANOTHER THREATENING PERIL

Loud cheers greeted the appearance of the seven scouts, as they hurried forward into the camp. And when those who had remained with the tents saw the various scratches, contusions and bumps that adorned most of the returned boys' faces, they were burning with eagerness to hear the details of the adventure.

Such a clatter of tongues as ensued, as every fellow tried to tell his version of the happening. If half that was said were written down, it would require many more chapters to give the details.

Gradually, however, each stay-at-home scout began to get a pretty clear idea of the series of adventures that had befallen their mates in trying to explore the mysteries of the island. They understood all about the wild man, and what the consensus among the seven explorers seemed to be concerning the strangers who occupied the island, and were conducting such an amazing series of experiments, even making use of an aeroplane to accomplish their ends.

The guesses that followed were legion, yet Paul, who listened patiently to the most astounding theories, shook his head in the end.

"I don't believe any of us have hit on the right thing yet, fellows," he said. "But there's meat in a number of the guesses you've made, and perhaps we'll get the story after a while. But how about grub; we're as hungry as bears?"

"Never expected to join you at lunch, for a fact," grinned Bobolink; "but then, we made better time than we ever thought we could on the return journey. Talk to me about a prize spurrin' a fellow on to do his level best - the whip that does it is to put a first-class scare in him. Then you're goin' to see some runnin' that takes the cake. Wheel didn't we sprint, though? Bet you I jumped clear over a log that stood six feet high from the ground - more or less."

It happened that the stay-at-home scouts had just prepared their noon meal at the time the explosion occurred that made the whole island tremble. That had startled them so much that they had not had the heart to think of sitting down because of anxiety about the fate of their chums.

And so the dinner had remained untouched up to the time they heard the "cooee" of the returning warriors; and then caught the bark of the fox, that told them that Paul and his posse had returned.

There was enough for all, because the cooks were very liberal in making up their messes. And over the dinner more suggestions were made as to what their future course ought to be.

By now even the fire-eating Bobolink was ready to cry quits, and back down; nor did he seem at all ashamed to admit the fact that he was afraid.

"If those sillies mean to blow up the whole island, some way or other, why, what's the use of us stayin' here, an' goin' up with it, I'd like to know?" he said. "Tell you what, I've got another guess comin', and it's this: P'raps they're meanin' to get rid of this island and lake, and have started to do the job. Mebbe some big railroad wants a short line across country, and this thing is right in their way. I've heard of 'em doin' bigger things than just blowing up a little island; haven't you, Paul?"

He always appealed to the scout master when one of his brilliant thoughts came along. Paul nodded his head.

"That sounds more reasonable than a whole lot of things I've been listening to, Bobolink, for a fact," Paul admitted. "Still, we don't know, and there's no way to find out the true story, right now. Listen, fellows!"

"Thunder, away off, Paul; guess we've all got explosions on the brain, because it gave me a start, too," said Jack, laughing.

"And if a storm's coming along," observed Jud Elderkin, who seemed vastly pleased when he heard that his signalling had been so easily understood, "why, I reckon we ought not to think of pulling down our good tents, and getting out of here, till she's over."

It was plain from this that the scouts had determined to abandon their dangerous island, and spend the balance of the outing by making a camp on the mainland, where at least there was a reasonable expectation of not being blown sky-high by some explosion.

"And since we're done eating perhaps we'd better take another look at the tent pins, to make sure they'll hold when the wind strikes us. Some of these summer storms have a lively advance breeze, you know, boys," Paul suggested.

"Little Billie and I'll go over to the boats, and see that the curtains are buttoned down snug. Some of us can stay inside while its rainin' and that'll give more room in the tents," Bobolink remarked, jumping to his feet, with a return of his customary lively Way.

"And in this sink we'll be protected from any wind coming from the south, don't you think, Paul?" Jack ventured.

"Couldn't be better," was the reply. "Those trees and bushes, as well as the rise in the ground, will help a lot. But get busy, fellows, with those tent pins. I'll take the axe, and go the rounds myself, to make doubly sure. It's not the nicest thing in the world to have your canvas blow away - eh, Nuthin?"

"You're right, it isn't," replied the little scout, "'specially when it lifts you right up with it into a tree, and has you tied up there in the snarls of a clothes line. I know all about that, and none of the rest of you ever tried it. Excuse me from another balloon ride like that."

In a short time everything was done that could be thought of to render things storm-proof. Then the boys went over to the edge of the water to watch the advance of the black clouds, which those at the boats in the little cove declared was a sight worth seeing.

And it certainly was, all the scouts admitted. Some of them were filled with a certain awe, as they saw how inky the clouds looked. But what boy, or man either, for that matter, is there who has not felt this sensation when watching scurrying clouds that tell of an approaching storm?

By degrees the boys began to drift back to the camp. Every sort of excuse was given for leaving the beach. One fellow suddenly remembered that he had left his coat hanging on a bush, another had forgotten to fasten his knapsack, while a third wished to tie his blanket in a roll, in case the water did find a way to get into the sink.

Paul, Jack, Bobolink and Jud remained until they saw the rough water away down near the southern shore of the lake, and understood that the first squall must be swooping upon them. Then they too gave up the vigil, for the chances were the rain would come with the first breeze.

With a howl and a roar the storm broke upon them. Cowering in the tents, about four in each, as the others had taken to the boats, they waited with more or less suspense what might happen.

The wind made the canvas shake at a lively clip, and the fastenings on the southern side were sorely tried; but they had been well taken care of and Paul called out that he believed they were going to hold.

For half an hour the rain beat down in torrents. None of them remembered ever hearing such a deluge descend, but perhaps their imaginations were excited on account of the peculiar conditions that surrounded them. All the same it rained, and then rained some more, until a very large quantity of water must have fallen, all of them decided.

With Paul and Jack in the tent that was nearest to the lake were Bobolink, Tom Betts and Nuthin.

"Seems to me it's gettin' kind of damp in here," remarked Bobolink, when the clamor outside had died down somewhat, and they could hear each other talk.

"That's a fact," declared Paul; "and after all it's just as well that we made sure our blankets and other things were tied up and hung away from the ground. But seems to me I hear one of the fellows in the boat shouting to us."

When he opened the flap he found that the rain had almost stopped, as well as the wind to a great extent. Perhaps the storm was over.

"Hello!" Paul called out.

"Hey! that you, Paul?" came in a voice he recognized as belonging to Jud, who had been one of those in charge of the nearby boats.

"Yes, what's wrong?" asked the scout master.

"Can't you come over here? Going to be the dickens to pay, I reckon. The bally old lake's rising like fun. Looks like the outlet must have got stopped up somehow. You're sure going to have to move your tents mighty quick. Coming, Paul?"

"All right," answered the other, as he crawled out, and started under the dripping trees for the spot where the two motorboats lay in the cove, sheltered from the waves that had been dashing against the shore elsewhere.

When he reached the spot he found that all of the boys who had been sheltered in the boats were lined up on the shore, where they could see down the lake. Jud himself seemed to be watching the water steal up a stick he had thrust into the sand.

"Gee! she's mounting like fun!" he exclaimed. "Water must be pouring into the old lake from every side, and little gettin' out. Say, if this keeps on, the whole island, except that hill up yonder, will be under water before night. It sets rather low, you understand, Paul."

The scout master was naturally thrilled by these words. He knew that the leader of the Gray Fox Patrol was no alarmist, and that he seldom lost his head in times of excitement.

And so it was with considerable apprehension that Paul stooped down so he might see just how fast the lake was rising. And when he noticed that it actually crept up the stick before his very eyes, he knew that what Jud had said about the whole island being covered might not be such a silly assertion after all.

It began to look as though the adventures of the scouts had not yet reached an end, and that they were in for another thrilling experience.

CHAPTER XXVIII

PREPARED FOR THE WORST

"She's just walking up hand over fist; eh, Paul?" asked Jud.

"No question about it, Jud," came the reply as the scout master cast an apprehensive look across the half-mile of water that separated them from the outlet of the lake. "I'd give something to know what's happened down there, to dam this water up, and just how far it's going to rise on us."

"Tell you what," said Bobolink, who had followed Paul when he left the tent, as had also the rest of the occupants, "I wouldn't be a bit surprised if that awful explosion shook the shoulder of earth and rock down, that we saw hanging above the mouth of the Radway River where she leaves the lake."

"You've hit it, I do believe!" cried Paul, exultantly; "and that's just what did happen, chances are, fellows."

"But if the outlet is filled up," said Jud, "and this water keeps pouring in on four sides, it's dead sure the blooming lake will fill up in short order. What had we better do, Paul?"

"That's just what I'm trying to figure on, Jud," answered the other; "it's one of two things - either hike out for the hill, where we'll be safe until the water goes down; or else get our things aboard the boats, and stay here."

"That last strikes me as the best of all!" declared Jack.

"Besides," broke in Nuthin, "we don't want to lose those boats, you know. They were loaned to us and if we let 'em go to smash, wouldn't it take us a long time to pay the bill, though? Besides, we'll need 'em to get away from here."

"That isn't the worst of it," remarked Paul, who was very serious.

"Why, what is there besides?" demanded Bobolink.

"Suppose the water does get up so as to cover the island, all but the hill," the scout master went on deliberately, as though making sure of his ground as he talked; "and then, all of a sudden the weight of it broke through the dam; don't you see the suction, as the water rushed out, would be something *terrific*. No rope ever made, I reckon, could hold these boats back. They'd sure be drawn through the gap, and carried on the flood, any old way, even upside-down, maybe."

"Whew!" whistled Bobolink; and as for some of the other fellows, they began to lose their usual color as they realized what Paul was saying.

"Now, that's just an idea that came into my mind," Paul went on, seeing that he had alarmed some of the scouts. "It may never happen, you understand. But you know the motto we believe in is 'be prepared!' That means never to take things for granted. Keep your eyes and ears always on guard, and see lots of things, even before they swoop down on you. So, it's up to us, fellows, to get our tents and other fixings loaded up as soon as we can. After that we'll go aboard ourselves, and try to prepare against a sudden break in the dam."

"And lookin' at that water creeping up," remarked Jud, "the sooner we get busy, the better."

Accordingly, they all hastened back to the camp. It was found that already the water seemed to be creeping into the sink. Those in the other two tents were talking it over, and wondering what was about to happen.

When they heard the latest news, their faces indicated both astonishment and not a little alarm. But under the direction of the scout master, they started to convey all their belongings to the boats.

First the blankets and clothes bags were taken over; then the food and cooking utensils; and finally the tents came down in a hurry, for the boys were working in water almost up to their knees when this last part of the job was concluded.

Once out of the sink, they found plenty of high ground to walk on, while carrying the wet tents to the landing where the boats were lying.

After they were all aboard, the scouts packed the stuff as best they could, so that it would take up as little space as possible. Meanwhile Paul and Jack, with both the other patrol leaders, were trying to figure out just what would be the best course for them to pursue.

"Makes me think of old Noah, when he went aboard the ark, and the animals they followed two by two," said Bobolink, with a chuckle.

"Huh, call yourself a kangaroo, or a monkey, if you like," spoke up Old Dan Tucker, "but as for me I'd rather play the part of Ham, or one of the other sons."

"Sure thing!" assented Bobolink, cheerfully; "never saw the time yet when you raised any kick about takin' the part of Ham. Sounds good, don't it, Dan?"

It was pretty hard to keep the spirits of Bobolink from sizzling and gushing forth like a fountain when the water is turned on. He could joke, even while the several leaders of the expedition were consulting gravely about their chances of holding the boats against the frightful suction of the current, when the obstructions in the outlet of the lake gave way, which they hoped would not be suddenly, but by degrees.

It was certainly a condition that confronted them, and not a theory. Paul was really more worried than he showed; for he kept his feelings under control, knowing that if some of the others realized how much he was concerned, the fact might create a panic.

"If I really thought the worst would come," Paul said, in a low tone, to Jack, after it had been concluded that they would stay by the boats, and do the best they could, "why I'd be tempted to give the order to just cut for the hill, and leave everything but some food behind. Once up there, we would be safe, and that's what we can't say is the case now."

"But even if the water goes out with a rush, it can't tear a tree like this one up by the roots; can it?" asked Jack, pointing to where the cables of the boats had been secured as strongly as possible.

"That's so," replied the scout master; "but then, think of the ropes, and what a terrible strain would come on them. I'm afraid both would snap like pipe-stems. To hold tight, we'd need a big chain; or a hawser like that one the switching engine on the railroad uses to drag cars on a parallel track. But then, the water may be nearly as high, right now, as it will get We'll hope so, anyhow."

That was Paul's way of trying to look on the bright side, although he never failed to prepare for the worst, even while expecting the best.

"If we could only think up some way to help ease the strain, it would be a good thing," observed Jack, thoughtfully.

"I wish you could. It would ease my mind more than I care to tell you," was Paul's answer.

"One thing, the storm is over," called out Jud, just then; "see, there's a break in the clouds, and I reckon the sun will be peepin' out soon."

"But the water will keep on rushing down the sides of the hills away off yonder," Paul remarked, "and filling up this cup until it runs over. They say that the Radway River drains three times the amount of country that our own Bushkill does. And by the way the water comes in here, I believe it. Look out there on the lake, will you; it shows that it's getting wider right now."

"Why, in another half hour, if it keeps on the same way, it's going to lap over pretty much all the lower part of the island," Jack declared.

Everything else was neglected now, and the scouts gathered along the side of each boat, watching the lake. It was as if they half expected to see the water suddenly take to rushing toward the spot where they knew the peculiar outlet lay, not more than twenty feet across, and with abrupt sides, one of which had been partly overhanging the water at the time they entered.

It was, of course, this section which must have been dislodged by the blast which shook the surrounding territory, filling the bed of the stream, and causing the rapidly accumulating waters of the lake to back up, since they could find no place to discharge, as usual.

It was while they were moodily watching the waste of waters that one of the scouts, who had wandered across to the other side of the *Comfortt* suddenly sounded a fresh alarm, that sent another thrill to the hearts of the already excited boys.

"Hey! here's a lot of men comin' down on us, fellows I They're meanin' to capture our boats, just like pirates. Boarders ahoy! Get busy everybody. Clubs are trumps!"

George A. Warren

As they rushed to the other side, some having to clamber over the heaps of duffle that took up so much room aboard, the scouts saw that it was no false alarm. A number of men were hurrying toward them, splashing through water that was in places almost knee deep, even when they took the upper levels. Should they make a blunder, and stray off the ridges, it was likely they would speedily have to swim for it.

Paul was considerably aroused at first. They did not know very much about these mysterious people of the island; and after their recent rough experience, most of the boys were decidedly averse to knowing anything more of them. And yet, here they were hurrying toward the two motor-boats, as though they might indeed have some desperate idea in view.

Perhaps they meant to capture the boats, so as to insure their escape from the rising waters. And then again, it seemed at least possible that they might want to keep the scouts from telling what strange things they had seen.

So the first thing Paul did when he had that glimpse of the oncoming men, was to hasten to possess himself of his double-barreled shotgun. Not that he expected that there would be any necessity for firing it, but it was apt to inspire a certain amount of respect.

And the balance of the scouts had made haste to arm themselves with whatever they could find that would help hold the enemy at bay. Some had brought their clubs aboard, others seized upon the push poles, while one grabbed up the camp axe, and another seized upon the hatchet.

When eighteen husky and determined lads line the sides of two boats, prepared to give a good account of themselves, it must needs be brave men who would dare try to clamber aboard.

And it was about this time, when things were looking rather squally around the floating homes of the scouts, that Paul noticed something singular.

CHAPTER XXIX

LIFTING THE LID

Three men could be seen splashing desperately through the water; and they seemed to be carrying a fourth, who was lying on a rude sort of litter, as though he might either be sick, or badly hurt.

And so it flashed through Paul's mind that perhaps after all their mission was not one of conquest, or even hostility, but that they were seeking help.

"Hold up, fellows," he hastened to say; "we'll have to let them come aboard now, because they never could get back to the hill again, with the water rising so fast. Besides, I think they've got a wounded man along, and need help. Don't forget we're scouts, and always ready to hold out a helping hand."

"That's the ticket!" declared the impulsive Bobolink, forgetting his warlike disposition when he saw the man on the litter.

So Paul beckoned to the men to approach. He had already made the discovery that one of those who bore the litter was the big man who had waved them away with such violent gestures, just before the terrible explosion, when they happened to get too near the mine that was being fired for some strange purpose.

Two minutes later, and still splashing through water that came almost up to their hips, those who bore the injured man arrived close to the boats.

"Why, it's Professor Hackett who's being carried!" exclaimed Jack.

The small man on the litter, who looked very white, lifted his head with an effort, and tried to wave his hand.

"Yes, that's who it is; and you're Jack Stormways; aren't you? Oh! I hope that chum of yours can do something to stop this bleeding; I made them carry me down here as a last chance. My man who was sent for a doctor in our aeroplane, has not come back, and we're afraid he had an accident. Can some of you boys help lift me aboard? I'm very weak from loss of blood, and nearly gone."

His voice was as faint as a whisper; and indeed, it was a wonder that he managed to speak at all.

The scouts had quite forgotten everything but that there was some one in trouble. Tender hands immediately were forth-coming to assist in raising litter and man over the side of the boat. Then the three attendants climbed aboard, and strange to say the scouts seemed to have forgotten all their fear of the men they had believed to be lawbreakers. For now they saw that they were an intelligent lot of men, who bore little resemblance to such criminals as they had seemed to be.

Paul had long been interested in surgery. His father was the leading doctor of Stanhope, and had always encouraged this fancy in the boy. It seemed that the professor chanced to remember that he had been told about the ability of Jack Stormways' chum; and when matters began to look desperate, since none of his assistants could seem to stop the flow of blood that followed his accident, as a last resort he had forced them to put him on a litter, and make for the spot where they knew the scouts had their camp, the man in the aeroplane having signaled the fact back to them, just as Paul suspected.

Of course they had not dreamed of such a thing as the lake rising, until they had gone too far to retreat; and then they took desperate chances of finding the boys still there, where they had boats with which they could go to the mainland.

Paul busied himself immediately. It was a pretty bad wound that the little man had received, and his left arm would be practically useless the balance of time; but he cared not for this, if only his life might be spared.

Jack and Jud assisted whenever their services were needed and in the end Paul had not only stopped the flow of blood, but had the injured arm neatly bandaged - as well, the professor weakly declared, as any surgeon could have done.

"And now," said Paul, turning on the big man, who had hovered around anxiously, watching what was being done, as though he thought a great deal of the professor; "in return for what we've done, won't you please tell us who and what you are, and why you're doing all these queer stunts away up here on this lonely island, where nobody can see you? We're all mixed up, and don't know what to think. At first we believed you must be a lot of counterfeiters hiding from the Government agents; but what with these explosions, and such things as aeroplanes, I'm getting it in my head that it means you're trying out some big sensations that are going to be sprung on the Coney Island public next season."

"And that's where you made a pretty clever guess, my boy," said the big man, as he settled down to take it a bit more easily after his recent hard work; "Professor Hackett has invented most of the biggest sensations seen at seaside resorts these last ten years. He expects to excel his record next season, and then retire; and I tell you, now, I began to think he'd retire another way, if he lost much more blood from that wound, which he got by accident this morning."

The scouts looked at each other, and a broad smile appeared on many a face that only a short time before had been pale with apprehension.

When a thing that has seemed a dark mystery is finally explained, it often looks so easy and simple that all of us wonder how we ever could have bothered our heads over such a puzzle. And so it was in this case. Why did it come that no one had guessed the true explanation before, when it was so easy?

They began to tell the big man all about their experiences, and how so many things seemed to make it appear that the strangers were hiding from officers.

"How about that fellow who was hanging around my father's mill that night you had your two big boxes stored there?" Jack asked.

"He represented a rival inventor, who has always been jealous of Professor Hackett, and is forever trying to find out what he has on the stocks," replied the big man, whose name they learned was Mr. Jameson, an able assistant to the inventor of aerial bombs, brilliant exploding mines, and a dozen other wonders that thrill audiences at the seashore each season.

"But wouldn't he be likely to follow the wagon when it took the boxes away in the morning?" the boy continued to ask.

"Oh! we put him on a false scent, by shipping two other boxes away on a train," was the reply. "He must have gone two hundred miles before he discovered his mistake; and I doubt very much if he knows yet, but is watching those cases to see what we do with them, away out in western New York State."

"Er, how about these?" asked Bobolink, jingling the two shining quarters in his hand. "I picked 'em up close to that field smithy you have on the island. We thought they were the best counterfeits we ever saw. I guess they are."

"I lost a bunch of small change through a hole in my pocket," laughed the man, "and so I judge those are a part of it. But keep them as souvenirs of your wonderful adventures on Cedar Island. Every time you look at them you'll remember that narrow escape you and your friends had when you came near stepping on a mine, the fuse of which had been lighted; for Professor Hackett, even while he was wounded, would not hear of us stopping our work."

"Thanks," replied the gratified Bobolink, again pocketing the quarters that had been the cause of so much speculation among the seven scouts; "I'll be glad to accept your kind offer. But there's another thing we'd like to know."

"Speak up, then, and I'll be pleased to accommodate you, if the knowledge is in my power to bestow. This flood bids fair to bring our experiments to an end for the time being, even if the professor's weakness hadn't made it necessary that we get to some place where he can receive the right kind of care, to build up his strength. What's bothering you now, my boy?"

"How about the wild man?" asked Bobolink.

"Oh! he was here when we came, and we made friends with him," the other replied, promptly. "You see, some of us have been up here for a month. We had some new stuff shipped in those big cases; but it'll all be rusted now by this water. The poor fellow is harmless, for all he looks so fierce. Why, at the smell of coffee the tears trickled down his dirty cheeks like rain; it seemed to be just one last link that bound his flitting memory to something in the far-away past. We gave him an old saucepan to cook it in, and showed him how. Ever since he's visited us often, and we supplied him with food, because it seemed as though he was the one who had first right to this island."

"I hope the poor old chap has the good sense to climb that hill, and get away from the rising water," remarked Jack, with some feeling. "Have you any idea who he can be, or where he came from?"

George A. Warren

"We made up our minds that he had been out of his head a long time, and perhaps had escaped from some institution. He mentioned the name of John Pennington once, and we think it must have been his. The professor intended to make inquiries, later on, and if possible have him returned to his home, wherever it might be."

"Did he have a big yellow dog tied up at his shack?" asked Nuthin, eagerly, as though he wished to settle that point, because the animal in question had once belonged to the Cypher family.

"Yes," answered Mr. Jameson, "but it got away from him one night, by breaking the rope, and he's been making a great fuss about it ever since. But from the ugly looks of the beast, I'd sooner put a bullet in him than try to make friends."

"Well, that about finishes the list of questions we've been nearly dying to ask somebody," remarked Bobolink, "and seems like everything's been explained. What we want to know now, and there isn't a livin' soul c'n tell the answer to that, I reckon, is, how high is this old lake goin' to get before she commences to fall again? And how in Sam Hill are we expectin' to ride those motor-boats over that pile of rocks and mud, that lies in the outlet? Anybody know the answer? I'd like to hear it."

But they shook their heads. Nobody could say, although all sorts of guesses ran the rounds, for the scouts were good hands at that sort of thing.

The water was still rising, and apparently just as fast as ever. Already it had encroached upon the main part of the island; and Mr. Jameson declared that he was sure it must be all around the shed where they kept their machinery, that had been brought secretly to this isolated spot, where they hoped to complete the greatest marvel in the way of sensations ever known to curious crowds at watering places.

"It'll be badly hurt, unless the water goes down soon," remarked the big man; "but that doesn't seem to be the worst thing that can happen, if what your Doctor Paul here, says, turns out to be true, and the water goes out of the lake in a raging torrent that may drag boats and all with it."

George A. Warren

CHAPTER XXX

GOOD-BYE TO CEDAR ISLAND

They passed a most anxious hour, after the coming of the professor and his assistants. The lake kept on rising until pretty much all of the island except the hill was under water. Of course the trees stood out, but most of their roots were under ten feet or more of water.

It would not last much longer, that they knew, for the supply must be falling short, and besides there was always a chance that the fearful force exerted by such a mass of pent-up water would break away the obstruction that clogged the outlet.

Paul had done everything he could think of to add to their security in case the worst came. Some of the scouts were even perched in the neighboring trees. These were the more timid, who Paul knew were shivering from anxiety, and watching the spot where the lake water ordinarily escaped, as though dreading lest at any second they should see a sudden heave that would mean the beginning of the end.

"Good news, Paul!" sang out Jud Elderkin, to whom had been delegated the duty of keeping watch on the rise of the flood. "She's stationary at last Never rose a bit the last ten minutes. And believe me, I honestly think she's begun to go down just a little."

The other boys let out a cheer at this news. That was what they were all hoping for - that the water would go down gradually, so as not to endanger the motorboats.

Just how the craft were to get out of the lake, if the exit remained closed, no one could say; but then they might look to Paul to open a way somehow. He could make use of some dynamite to blow up the obstructions, so Mr. Jameson had suggested, and it sounded all right.

Five minutes later Jud was quite positive that the tide was on the ebb.

"Two inches lower than she was at the highest point. Paul!" he called out, jubilantly.

"Hurrah! that sounds good to me!" exclaimed Bobolink, swinging his campaign hat vigorously about his head, as he sat in the bow of the *Comfort*, it being a part of his task to watch the cable, and if the worst came to ease up on it so that there would be less likelihood of a sudden snap.

"But we're not out of danger yet, remember," cautioned the scout master.

Presently the water was lowering at a still faster rate.

"Looks like the opening might be getting larger," said Jack, when this fact was made clear beyond any doubt.

"Watch over there," said Paul, "and see if there's any sudden rush, though already the water is escaping so fast that I begin to believe we might hold on here, even if the whole pile of earth and rocks were washed away, leaving the channel clear."

Five, ten, fifteen minutes crept along, and all the while the water kept going steadily down until much of the island could be seen again under the trees.

"Oh! look, there she goes!" cried Bobolink, without warning, and thereby causing some of the fellows who had descended from the trees to wish they were aloft again.

Over in the vicinity of the outlet they could see something of a commotion. The water seemed to be running down hill, as it struggled to pour out through the now cleared passage.

Immediately the boats felt the suction, which must have been very strong indeed. They strained at their ropes, and those who had the cables in charge obeyed the instructions given to them, allowing a certain length of line to slip, thus easing the fearful drag.

"Whoop! they're going to hold!" exclaimed Bobolink, in great glee.

Paul believed so himself, and a smile came to his face that up to now had looked careworn and anxious; for a dreadful catastrophe had been hovering over them, he felt certain.

And the ropes did make good, holding in spite of that fierce drag. The water soon got down to about its normal level, when the pull upon the hawsers ceased, and everything seemed to settle back into the old rut.

But the boys had had quite enough of Cedar Island. It was water-soaked now, and offered little attraction to them for camping. Paul suggested that they leave the cove and head for a certain section of the main shore which, on account of being much higher than the island, had not been overflowed.

There was not a single voice raised in opposition, and so they started the motors and with a series of derisive sounds that seemed almost like chuckles the boats said goodbye to Cedar Island. Landing they found a splendid spot for the erection of the tents, and before the coming of night the scouts were as snugly fixed as though nothing had happened to disturb them.

The injured professor declared that he meant to stick by Paul until his messenger arrived with a carriage and a doctor by way of the road, which ran only a half mile away from the lake.

He expressed himself satisfied with the work Paul had done on his arm, and believed it to be the right thing.

They hoped to spend a quiet night. There would be no bomb explosions in the heavens to disturb them, at least. Mr. Jameson had already explained to the boys that, if they had happened to be awake at the time of that first tremendous shock, they must have seen by the glare in the heavens that it was a new kind of aerial bomb that had been fired; and possibly under such conditions some one of the scouts would have guessed the truth. But when they crept out of the tents there was nothing to be seen aloft.

Luckily, these wide-awake boys could accommodate themselves to their surroundings. Their former experiences had made most of them quickwitted, resolute and cheerful under difficulties that might have daunted most lads.

Although they had received a tremendous shock because of the numerous remarkable occurrences that had taken place since their landing on Cedar Island, now that their troubles seemed to have departed, most of the scouts were just as full of life and good-natured "chaff" as ever.

Bluff seemed to never tire of entertaining those who had not been fortunate enough to be among the valiant band of explorers with wonderful accounts of all they had seen. He had them holding their very breath with awe, as he described, in his own way, how they first of all crept up to the shack in the thicket and looked in upon the wild man asleep.

But when Bluff told of how he and his comrades had been warned off in such a dramatic manner by the unknown man, and immediately afterwards found themselves knocked down by that tremendous concussion, as the explosion took place, he had them hanging on his every sentence.

But words failed Bluff when he tried to picture the wild scene that had followed. That furious scamper through the wooded part of the island must remain pretty much in the nature of a nightmare with the boys.

Phil and Bobolink and Andy all eagerly chimed in, trying to do the subject justice, but after all it seemed beyond their powers. They could only end by holding up both hands, rolling their eyes, shrugging their shoulders, and then mutely pointing to the various cuts, scratches and contusions that decorated their faces. The rest had to be left to the imagination.

Fortunately there was an abundance of witch hazel ointment along, so that every sufferer was able to anoint his hurts. The whole bunch seemed to fairly *glisten* from the time of their arrival at the boats. Indeed, there never had been such a wholesale raid made upon the medical department since the Stanhope Troup of Banner Boy Scouts was organized.

But after all was said and done they had come out of the whole affair at least with honor. And now that the peril was a thing of the past they could well afford to laugh at their adventures on Cedar Island.

CHAPTER XXXI

A SCOUT'S DUTY

"Seems like a dream; don't it, Paul?"

Jack dropped down beside the acting scout master as he made this remark. He had just stepped out from the new camp on the mainland, and found Paul sitting upon a log, looking across the water in the direction they had come.

The sun was just setting, and a rosy flush filled the western heavens. It seemed to fall softly upon mysterious Cedar Island, nestling there in the midst of the now tranquil waters.

Paul looked up with a smile, as he made room on the log for his chum, who had always been so willing to stand by him through thick and thin.

"Well, do you know, Jack," he spoke, "that was just exactly what seemed to strike me. I was staring hard at the island, and wondering if I had been asleep and dreamed all those queer happenings. Fact is, just before you spoke I even pinched my leg to see if I was really wide awake."

The other laughed at this.

"Oh! you're awake, all right, Paul," he remarked. "You seemed to get off without any show of damage to your good-looking face. As for the rest of us, if ever we begin to think we've been and dreamed it, we've got a remedy better than pinching. All we have to do is to bend down over a still pool of water and take a look at our faces. That'll convince us in a hurry we *did* have a lively time of it."

Paul pointed across the lake to where the island lay bathed in that wonderful afterglow that shone from the painted heavens.

"Did you ever see a prettier sight?" he asked. "It looks as peaceful as any picture could be. You wouldn't think a bunch of fellows could run up against such a lot of trouble over on such a fine little place as Cedar Island; would you, now?"

"I feel the same way you do, Paul; and I'd say we never ought to have left it, only after the flood it'd be a muddy place, and we wouldn't take any pleasure getting around."

"Oh! well," Paul rejoined cheerfully, "after all, perhaps it isn't our last visit up this way. Who knows but what we may have another chance to come over here and look around. It was a good scheme, I'm thinking, Jack, and we'll never be sorry we came."

"I should say not," remarked the other, quickly; "just turn around and take a look back into our camp. See where Professor Hackett is lying propped up with pillows from the boats. Well, suppose we'd never come over this way, what d'ye think would have happened to him? He says he owes his life to your skill, Paul, and that, try as they would, Mr. Jameson and the other assistants couldn't seem to stop the bleeding. That alone pays us for all we've gone through, Paul."

"I guess it does," Paul admitted, readily, "because he's a smart man, and has done a lot to entertain the crowds that go to the seashore to rest and forget their troubles. But I'm glad none of the boys seem to have suffered any serious damage from the effect of the explosion or that mad chase afterwards."

"Yes, we ought to call ourselves lucky, and let it go at that,"

Jack remarked.

"When you think about all that might have happened, I tell you we've got lots of reason to be thankful," Paul went on, with considerable feeling.

"Sure we have," added Jack. "Instead of that stick taking me in the cheek, it might have struck my eye and injured my sight for life."

"And where I got only a wrench that may make me limp a little for a few days, I could have broken a leg," said Paul.

"That's one of the rules scouts have to keep in mind, you know," Jack continued; "always be cheerful and look on the bright side of things. I reckon there never comes a time when you can't find a rainbow of promise if you look far enough. Things are never as bad as they might be."

"The boys seem to have settled down here just as if they meant to enjoy the rest of the stay," Paul observed, as he turned his head again, so as to look at the bustling camp close by.

"Yes, and even the very air seems to tell of peace and plenty," said Jack, with a little laugh, as he sniffed the appetizing odors that were beginning to announce that preparations for the evening meal had started.

"You're right," agreed Paul, "I guess there's nothing more 'homey' than the smell of onions frying. I never get a whiff of it on the street of a winter evening but what I seem to see some of the camps I've been in. And then, just think how it gets your appetite on edge, till you can hardly wait for the cook to call out that supper's ready. But I was thinking of some other things when you came up."

"I reckon I could mention one of them," said Jack.

"Let's hear, then," the other demanded.

Jack swept his hand down the lake in the direction of the outlet.

"You're worrying about that," he said.

"Well, that's just about the size of it, Jack. We know the lake's gone down to about what it was before the storm hit us; but what if a great big rock blocks the passage?"

"You know what Mr. Jameson said you could do?" Jack remarked.

"About the dynamite, to blast an opening big enough for our boats to get through? Yes, Jack, I suppose that could be done."

"And he says he'll stand by to see that it *is* done," the other continued. "As Mr. Jameson is an expert at all sorts of explosives, you can just make up your mind we'll have no trouble getting away. Besides, Paul, I've got a feeling that when we go down in the morning to take a survey, we'll be more than pleased with the way things look."

"Which all sounds good to me," Paul hastened to declare. "Anyhow, I'm going to believe it's bound to turn out as you say. In spite of our troubles we've been a pretty lucky lot."

"But you talked as though the getting away part of the business was only a part of what you had on your mind," Jack went on.

"There was something else," the other scout admitted.

"Suppose you open up and tell me, Paul; because somehow I don't seem to be able to get what you mean."

"It seems to me," the patrol leader remarked, seriously, "that while all of us scouts, and the professor's party in the bargain, have been shaking hands with each other over the lucky escape we had, we've pretty near forgotten one poor chap."

Jack gave a start, and then whistled softly.

"That's right, Paul," he said, "for I take it you mean the crazy islander."

"How do we know what happened to him?" Paul continued.

"But Mr. Jameson seemed to feel sure he would take to the hill when the flood came," Jack replied. "And he also told us, you remember, that some of their food was at a higher point than the water could have reached. So, if the crazy man wanders about that camp, there's no need of his going hungry long."

"I guess that's about so," Paul agreed, as though these words from his chum took away some of his anxiety. "From what they say, it seems as if he has come to look on them as friends. So, chances are ten to one he'd go to their different camps after the flood went down."

"Queer how he came to be here," Jack remarked.

"Oh, I don't know," the other observed; "there's no telling what a crazy person will do. His coming to this island must have been with the hazy notion that any one searching for him couldn't find him here."

"Searching for him, Paul?"

"Well, you remember Mr. Jameson said he had an idea the poor fellow must have escaped from some institution," Jack continued.

"Yes, he did say that; and for all he looks so big and fierce, with his long hair and beard, he's harmless. But, Jack, between us now, do you think we could go back home when our little vacation trip is over and feel that we'd done *all* our duty as true scouts, when that poor chap had been left up here - perhaps to starve on Cedar Island?"

"Whew! You're the greatest boy I ever saw, Paul, to get a grip on a situation and remember things."

"But - answer my question," persisted the other.

"Well, what you said must be so," Jack acknowledged; "and it makes me feel pretty small to remember that, while we've all been feeling so merry over our wonderful escape, I'd forgotten all about *him*."

"Jack, it's too late to do anything tonight, you know."

"I reckon it is, Paul," replied the other, looking a bit anxiously across the water to where the glow was commencing to give way to shadows along the wooded shore of Cedar Island; "but if you thought best, I'd be willing to take the lantern and cross over with you."

Paul thrust out his hand impulsively.

"Shake on that, old chum," he exclaimed. "Your heart's as big as a bushel basket, and in the right place every time. But on the whole, Jack, I don't believe it would be the wise thing for us to do."

"Just as you say, Paul; only I wanted you to know I was ready to back you up in anything."

"We're both tired, and sore in the bargain," continued the scout master, steadily.

"Yes," Jack admitted, unconsciously caressing his painful bruises.

"The island is in a bad state just now, after being flooded," Paul continued.

"That's right, I can jolly well believe it," his chum agreed.

"And if the wild man hasn't been drowned, he'll surely be able to look out for himself a while longer. Mr. Jameson felt sure he wouldn't starve, with all the food they left behind."

"Then it won't hurt to let it go till tomorrow, eh, Paul?"

"I had made up my mind that we'd organize another party, this time taking some of the fellows who have been kept in camp, and comb Cedar Island from end to end to find that man."

"A good plan, Paul," said the other scout; "but do you think he'll make friends with us, even when we find him?"

"Mr. Jameson says he understands the peace sign," the scout master continued, "and must really have had a bright mind at some time. He told me he had an idea the man may have met with some injury that had unsettled his reason. He seemed to be greatly interested in all they were doing, and several times even made suggestions that startled the professor."

"I remember that much, too," said Jack, "and Mr. Jameson also said he meant to try and learn if anybody knew about a John Pennington. That was the name the man spoke once in his rambling talk."

"Well, perhaps we may be able in some way to do the poor fellow a good turn, Jack. I hope so, anyhow. My! how those boys are trying to beat the record at getting up a grand supper. Seems to me my appetite is growing at the rate of a mile a minute."

"If it keeps on that way, good-bye to our stock of provisions," laughed Jack; "but, to tell the truth, I feel pretty much the same. The most welcome sound I could hear right now would be Bluff calling everybody to get a share of that fine mess."

"Then you won't have to wait long, I guess," his chum declared, "because from all the signs of dishing out I imagine they're about ready right now."

Paul proved a true prophet, for immediately Bluff began to ding-dong upon a sheet iron frying pan, using a big spoon to produce a discord that, in the ears of the hungry boys, was the sweetest music in the world.

Gathering around, the scouts made a merry group as they proceeded to demolish the stacks of savory food that had been heaped upon their tin plates; and drink to each other's health in the fragrant coffee that steamed in the generous cups, also of tin, belonging to their mess chest.

After supper the scouts sat around, and while some of them worked at various things in which they were particularly interested, such as developing the films that would give a dozen views of the great flood, others sang songs or listened to Mr. Jameson tell strange stories.

The man had been to the corners of the world during a busy lifetime, often with scientific parties sent out by societies interested in geography, natural history or astronomy. And hence it had fallen to the lot of Mr. Jameson to experience some remarkable adventures. The boys felt that he was the most interesting talker they had ever met.

After several hours had slipped by, some of the scouts, notably those who had been among the bold explorers band, were discovered to be nodding drowsily. Indeed, Andy and Tom Betts had gone sound asleep, just as they lay curled up before the fire. The warmth of the blaze, together with the unusual exertions of the day, had been too much for the boys.

And so the bugler was told to sound "taps" to signify that it was time they crawled under their blankets.

A few chose to sleep aboard the motor boats, which, of course, relieved the tents from overcrowding. Professor Hackett and his assistants had been lodged in one of the tents, which fact had something to do with the lack of room.

But presently all these things had been arranged. Paul himself intended to pass the night in the open. He declared he would really enjoy the experience; and two others insisted on keeping him company - little Nuthin and Bobolink.

So Paul, who knew a lot about these things, showed them just how to wrap themselves up like mummies in their blankets, and then lie with their feet to the fire. He said old hunters and cowboys always slept that way when camping in the open.

CHAPTER XXXII

CONCLUSION

Paul was awakened by feeling something nudging him in the ribs. It was Bobolink's elbow; and, thinking at first that it might be an accident, the scout master made no move.

But again he received a severe jolt. And at the same time came a whisper close in his ear:

"Paul! Are you awake?" Bobolink was saying, so low that any one six feet away could not have heard his voice.

"What ails you?" asked Paul.

He might have imagined that the other had been taken ill, from over feeding, perhaps, and wanted Paul, as the doctor of the troop, to give him some medicine. But on second thought Paul realized that there was too much mystery about the action of Bobolink to admit of such an explanation.

"Listen, Paul," the other went on, still whispering, "there's some sort of wild beast goin' to raid the camp!"

"What's that?" asked the scout master, a little sternly, for, knowing the weakness of Bobolink in the line of practical joking, he suspected that the other might be up to some of his old tricks.

And Bobolink must have detected an air of doubt in the manner in which Paul spoke those two words, for he immediately resumed:

"Honest Injun, Paul, I ain't foolin'! Say, do they have panthers around here? Because that's what I think it must be."

"Where'd you see it?"

As Paul put this question he was working his arms free from the folds of his blanket. When he lay down, more through force of habit than because he thought there would be any need of such a thing, Paul had placed his shotgun on the ground beside him. And no sooner was his right hand at liberty than, groping around, he took possession of it.

"Up in that big oak tree," Bobolink went on. "You watch where that limb hangs out over the camp and you'll see somethin' move; or I've been dreamin', that's all."

Paul did not have to twist his head very far around in order to see the spot in question. He watched it as the seconds began to troop along, until almost a fell minute had gone.

And Paul was just about to believe Bobolink must have been dreaming, when he, too, saw the bunch of leaves violently agitated.

Undoubtedly some tree-climbing animal was up there. Paul felt a thrill pass through him. Unconsciously, perhaps, his fingers tightened their grip upon the shotgun, which was apt to prove a tower of strength in case the worst that could happen came to pass.

Straining his eyes, as he partly lifted his head, Paul believed he could just make out a shadowy form stretched upon the large oak limb.

He was more than puzzled.

Wild animals were not altogether unknown within the twenty-mile limit around Stanhope. A bear might be seen occasionally - or at least the tracks of one, for the timid beast knew enough to hide in the daytime in one of the numerous swamps.

But this did not seem large enough for a bear, which would have surely made a more bulky object clinging to the limb. Moreover, bears were not reckoned bold, and no hunter had ever known one to come spying around a camp. As soon as the trail of human beings is run across by a bear, the animal always takes the alarm and hastens to its den, to lie low until the danger has passed.

But Bobolink had mentioned the magic word "panther," and this caused the other aroused scout to look more closely at the dimly seen object Sure enough it did seem to be flattened out on the limb, much as Paul imagined a big cat might lie.

"What'd we better do about it, Paul - give a yell and jump up?" Bobolink asked, his voice quivering, perhaps with excitement, or it might be under stress of alarm; for it was not the nicest thing in the world to be lying there helpless with a hungry panther crouching above.

"Wait, and let's make sure," replied the careful Paul.

Some impetuous boys would have thought, the very first thing, of bringing that double-barrelled gun to bear on the dark, shadowy figure, and cutting loose, perhaps even firing both charges at once.

At such close range, less than thirty feet, a shell containing even bird shot is apt to be projected with all the destructive qualities of a large bullet. Paul knew all about this, and also had faith in the hard-hitting qualities of his long tested gun; but he was not the one to be tempted into any rash action.

"Be sure you're right; then go ahead," was a motto which Paul always tried to practice. He had certainly found it worth while on more than one occasion in the past, and it was likely to serve him well now.

And so he waited, ready for a sudden emergency, but not allowing himself to be hurried.

He soon had reason to feel very thankful that his good sense had prevailed, for presently the leaves were again set to shaking and, as they parted, Paul saw something that gave him a shock.

"Oh! what d'ye think of that, now? It's the wild man of Cedar Island!" gasped Bobolink, actually sitting up in his excitement.

And Paul had already made certain of this fact as soon as his eyes fell upon the hairy face seen among the branches. The shudder that passed through his frame had nothing to do with fear. Paul was only horrified to realize what might have happened had he taken Bobolink's suggestion for the truth, and fully believed the figure in the oak to be a savage panther.

"We'd better let Mr. Jameson know," Paul remarked, as he also sat up and cleared his legs of the blanket.

"Yes, he'll know how to get him down. I bet you, Paul, the feller went and swam across from the island. But how would he guess we were here?"

"Oh! he could see the boats in the day time; and don't forget we've had a fire burning all night, so far," said the scout master.

When Mr. Jameson came out of the tent, in answer to Paul's low summons, and learned what had happened, he readily agreed to influence the wild man to come down. The poor fellow had learned to look on Mr. Jameson as a friend, and, realizing that he had abandoned the island, doubtless it was his desire to see him again that had induced this visit.

He proved to be harmless, and upon being given food ate

ravenously. Later on it was discovered that he had launched a log and made his way to the mainland by means of this crude craft, with a branch for a paddle.

Mr. Jameson declared that he would take the stranger to Stanhope when the vehicle came for the professor, and do all in his power to learn just who he was, as well as get him safely back among his friends.

To dispose of the wild man of Cedar Island once and for all, it might be said right here that Mr. Jameson kept his word. The name John Pennington served as a clue, and in the end he learned that was his name. He had lost his mind through an accident and, though his case was deemed hopeless, occasionally he was apt to have little flashes of his former cleverness. He was returned to the sanitarium from which he had escaped, and the boys never heard of him again. But the memory of the wild man would always be associated with Cedar Island.

On the following day Paul and Jack managed to get around to the outlet, for the scout master was anxious to learn what the chances of their leaving the lake, when they were ready, might be.

They found that, just as had been believed that shoulder of rock and earth had been shaken loose by the tremor of the earth at the time of the big shock, when the professor was experimenting with some new explosive.

In falling, it had indeed dammed the outlet, and the storm coming so soon after, of course the water in the lake had risen at a frightful rate. In the end the obstruction had commenced to disappear; but luckily for all concerned, it had held fairly well until much of the water had escaped, when finally it had given way.

The channel was as good as ever; indeed, Paul seemed to think that it offered fewer impediments to a passage now than before all this had happened.

That eased the minds of the scouts, and they could go back again to their camp with good news for the others.

A carriage came that day for the professor, and his assistants managed to carry him across country to the road; just as they had undoubtedly done the two big boxes of material that came from Mr. Stormways' mill that other day.

He shook hands with each and every scout before leaving, and promised to remember them always for what they had done. When he came to Paul, he clung to his hand, and there were tears in the eyes of the little professor as he, said:

"I honestly believe that you saved my life, my boy, and I trust that through your ability I may be spared a few more years. And depend on it, I'm never going to let you get out of touch with me, Paul Morrison. I hope to live to see you a great surgeon, some day."

The scouts filled out the balance of their vacation at the lake, and considered that they had had some of the strangest experiences that could happen to a group of boys; but although at the time they could not suspect it, there were still more interesting things in store for Paul and his comrades of Stanhope Troop of Boy Scouts. What these were, you will find related in the next volume of this series, to be called, "The Banner Boy Scouts Snowbound; Or, A Tour on Skates and Iceboats."

When the time came for them to start back, it was with more or less anxiety that they came to the canal connecting the waters of the two rivers flowing parallel for a few miles, and only a short distance apart.

But they need not have borrowed trouble, for the Bushkill was still higher than usual at this season of the year and all through the disused canal they found plenty of water, so that neither of the boats stuck in the mud.

In good time, then, the Banner Boy Scouts arrived home, to thrill the lads who had not been fortunate enough to accompany them on their trip afloat, with wonderful accounts of all the remarkable things which had happened to them while in camp on Cedar Island.

Choose from Thousands of 1stWorldLibrary Classics By

Ada Leverson
Adolphus William Ward
Aesop
Agatha Christie
Alexander Aaronsohn
Alexander Kielland
Alexandre Dumas
Alfred Gatty
Alfred Ollivant
Alice Duer Miller
Alice Turner Curtis
Alice Dunbar
Ambrose Bierce
Amelia E. Barr
Andrew Lang
Andrew McFarland Davis
Andy Adams
Anna Sewell
Annie Besant
Annie Hamilton Donnell
Annie Payson Call
Annonaymous
Anton Chekhov
Arnold Bennett
Arthur Conan Doyle
Arthur M. Winfield
Arthur Ransome
Atticus
B.H. Baden-Powell
B. M. Bower
Baroness Emmuska Orczy
Baroness Orczy
Basil King
Bayard Taylor
Ben Macomber
Bertha Muzzy Bower
Bjornstjerne Bjornson
Booth Tarkington
Boyd Cable
Bram Stoker
C. Collodi
C. E. Orr
C. M. Ingleby
Carolyn Wells
Catherine Parr Traill
Charles A. Eastman
Charles Dickens
Charles Dudley Warner
Charles Farrar Browne

Charles Ives
Charles Kingsley
Charles Klein
Charles Lathrop Pack
Charles Whibley
Charles Willing Beale
Charlotte M. Braeme
Charlotte M. Yonge
Charlotte Perkins Stetson
Clair W. Hayes
Clarence Day Jr.
Clarence E. Mulford
Clemence Housman
Confucius
Cornelis DeWitt Wilcox
Cyril Burleigh
D. H. Lawrence
Daniel Defoe
David Garnett
Don Carlos Janes
Donald Keyhoe
Dorothy Kilner
Dougan Clark
Douglas Fairbanks
E. Nesbit
E.P.Roe
E. Phillips Oppenheim
Edgar Rice Burroughs
Edith Van Dyne
Edith Wharton
Edward J. O'Biren
Edward S. Ellis
Edwin L. Arnold
Eleanor Atkins
Eliot Gregory
Elizabeth Gaskell
Elizabeth McCracken
Elizabeth Von Arnim
Ellem Key
Emerson Hough
Emily Dickinson
Enid Bagnold
Enilor Macartney Lane
Erasmus W. Jones
Ernie Howard Pie
Ethel Turner
Ethel Watts Mumford
Eugenie Foa
Eugene Wood

Evelyn Everett-green
Everard Cotes
F. H. Cheley
F. J. Cross
Federick Austin Ogg
Ferdinand Ossendowski
Francis Bacon
Francis Darwin
Frances Hodgson Burnett
Frances Parkinson Keyes
Frank Gee Patchin
Frank Harris
Frank Jewett Mather
Frank L. Packard
Frank V. Webster
Frederic Stewart Isham
Frederick Trevor Hill
Frederick Winslow Taylor
Friedrich Kerst
Friedrich Nietzsche
Fyodor Dostoyevsky
G.A. Henty
G.K. Chesterton
Gabrielle E. Jackson
Garrett P. Serviss
Gaston Leroux
George Ade
Geroge Bernard Shaw
George Durston
George Ebers
George Eliot
George MacDonald
George Meredith
George Orwell
George Tucker
George W. Cable
George Wharton James
Gertrude Atherton
Grace E. King
Grace Gallatin
Grant Allen
Guillermo A. Sherwell
Gulielma Zollinger
Gustav Flaubert
H. A. Cody
H. B. Irving
H.C. Bailey
H. G. Wells
H. H. Munro

H. Irving Hancock	James DeMille	Louisa May Alcott
H. Rider Haggard	James Joyce	Lucy Fitch Perkins
H. W. C. Davis	James Lane Allen	Lucy Maud Montgomery
Hamilton Wright Mabie	James Lane Allen	Lydia Miller Middleton
Hans Christian Andersen	James Oliver Curwood	Lyndon Orr
Harold Avery	James Oppenheim	M. Corvus
Harold McGrath	James Otis	M. H. Adams
Harriet Beecher Stowe	James R. Driscoll	Margaret E. Sangster
Harry Houidini	Jane Austen	Margaret Vandercook
Helent Hunt Jackson	Jens Peter Jacobsen	Margret Penrose
Helen Nicolay	Jerome K. Jerome	Maria Edgeworth
Hendrik Conscience	John Burroughs	Maria Thompson Daviess
Hendy David Thoreau	John Cournos	Mariano Azuela
Henri Barbusse	John F. Kennedy	Marion Polk Angellotti
Henrik Ibsen	John Gay	Mark Overton
Henry Adams	John Glasworthy	Mark Twain
Henry Ford	John Habberton	Mary Austin
Henry Frost	John Joy Bell	Mary Catherine Crowley
Henry James	John Kendrick Bangs	Mary Cole
Henry Jones Ford	John Milton	Mary Hastings Bradley
Henry Seton Merriman	John Philip Sousa	Mary Roberts Rinehart
Henry W Longfellow	Jonas Lauritz Idemil Lie	Mary Rowlandson
Herbert A. Giles	Jonathan Swift	M. Wollstonecraft Shelley
Herbert N. Casson	Joseph A. Altsheler	Maud Lindsay
Herman Hesse	Joseph Carey	Max Beerbohm
Homer	Joseph Conrad	Myra Kelly
Honore De Balzac	Joseph E. Badger Jr	Nathaniel Hawthrone
Horace Walpole	Joseph Hergesheimer	Nicolo Machiavelli
Horatio Alger Jr.	Joseph Jacobs	O. F. Walton
Howard Pyle	Julian Hawthrone	Oscar Wilde
Howard R. Garis	Julies Vernes	Owen Johnson
Hugh Lofting	Justin Huntly McCarthy	P.G. Wodehouse
Hugh Walpole	Kakuzo Okakura	Paul and Mabel Thorne
Humphry Ward	Kenneth Grahame	Paul G. Tomlinson
Ian Maclaren	Kenneth McGaffey	Paul Severing
Inez Haynes Gillmore	Kate Langley Bosher	Percy Brebner
Irving Bacheller	Kate Langley Bosher	Peter B. Kyne
Israel Abrahams	Katherine Cecil Thurston	Plato
Ivan Turgenev	Katherine Stokes	R. Derby Holmes
J.G.Austin	L. A. Abbot	R. L. Stevenson
J. Henri Fabre	L. T. Meade	R. S. Ball
J. M. Barrie	L. Frank Baum	Rabindranath Tagore
J. Macdonald Oxley	Latta Griswold	Rahul Alvares
J. S. Fletcher	Laura Lee Hope	Ralph Henry Barbour
J. S. Knowles	Laurence Housman	Ralph Waldo Emmerson
J. Storer Clouston	Leo Tolstoy	Rene Descartes
Jack London	Leonid Andreyev	Rex Beach
Jacob Abbott	Lewis Carroll	Rex E. Beach
James Allen	Lilian Bell	Richard Harding Davis
James Andrews	Lloyd Osbourne	Richard Jefferies
James Baldwin	Louis Tracy	Richard Le Gallienne

Robert Barr
Robert Frost
Robert Gordon Anderson
Robert L. Drake
Robert Lansing
Robert Lynd
Robert Michael Ballantyne
Robert W. Chambers
Rosa Nouchette Carey
Rudyard Kipling
Samuel B. Allison
Samuel Hopkins Adams
Sarah Bernhardt
Selma Lagerlof
Sherwood Anderson
Sigmund Freud
Standish O'Grady
Stanley Weyman
Stella Benson
Stephen Crane
Stewart Edward White
Stijn Streuvels
Swami Abhedananda

Swami Parmananda
T. S. Ackland
T. S. Arthur
The Princess Der Ling
Thomas A. Janvier
Thomas A Kempis
Thomas Anderton
Thomas Bailey Aldrich
Thomas Bulfinch
Thomas De Quincey
Thomas H. Huxley
Thomas Hardy
Thomas More
Thornton W. Burgess
U. S. Grant
Valentine Williams
Various Authors
Victor Appleton
Virginia Woolf
Walter Camp
Walter Scott
Washington Irving
Wilbur Lawton

Wilkie Collins
Willa Cather
Willard F. Baker
William Dean Howells
William le Queux
W. Makepeace Thackeray
William W. Walter
Winston Churchill
Yei Theodora Ozaki
Yogi Ramacharaka
Young E. Allison
Zane Grey